VAMPIRE ASH

SCORNED BY BLOOD, BOOK TWO

HEATHER RENEE

ISBN: 979-8775547882

Line Editing and Proofing: Jamie from Holmes Edits

Cover: Covers by Juan

Character Art: @kalynne_art on Instagram

Chapter Images: Samaiya Art

VAMPIRE ASH

CONTENTS

CHAPTER 1

SIX DAYS OF LIVING IN HELL WAS THE ONLY WAY I COULD describe my time spent since Silas drained most of the blood from my body. Something I planned to never let happen again.

Rachel had given me a transfusion, assuming since I was technically human that there wouldn't be a problem as long as she used the right blood type. She'd been wrong. My body had been furious about the intrusion of the foreign blood and seemed determined to make me pay for my actions.

First, there had been body chills so severe that my back spasmed uncontrollably and I couldn't get out of bed. Then came the fainting and dizziness, followed by a fever that rose so high, my muscles seized up for a solid day until I spent two hours in an ice bath to lower my temperature.

Rachel and Nikki were by my side through every wave of torture. My appreciation for them had grown tenfold while my feelings for Maciah had become muddled.

He hadn't come to see me. Not a single time. I should have expected it after the way he'd walked away from me once Silas was gone.

I didn't want to admit it out loud, but I was hurting. My chest tightened every time I heard heavy footsteps coming down the hallway, and my heart formed another crack when Maciah didn't appear in my doorway.

Though, whatever was happening between us—whatever he was upset about—would be figured out today. I'd woken up feeling normal for the first time in days. Maciah couldn't ignore me any longer. Not until I'd said my piece.

The sound of Rachel humming caught my attention as I headed to my closet. The tune was low and something I wouldn't have been able to hear just a week ago. My senses had been heightened over the last few days, and I wasn't sure that was a good thing.

"Good morning, Sunshine," Rachel called from the doorway.

"Morning. I'm getting dressed," I replied from inside my closet.

She jumped onto my bed and lay down, propping her head up with both hands while watching me.

"Creeper," I joked while looking for a shirt to wear. I'd been mostly unclothed while I was recovering. I wanted to find an outfit to lift my mood and make me feel good before I left my room.

She scoffed. "I'm pretty sure after all the times I've seen you naked, we've entered into official bestie zone, which means there can be no creepiness about me or my actions."

She really wasn't wrong about that.

"I was coming to see what you wanted for breakfast. Are you sure it's a good idea to be out of bed already?" Rachel asked as I slipped a black V-neck ribbed sweater over my head. February had arrived, and it was cold as hell outside, so long sleeves for the win.

"I promise I'm all better. No fever, aches, or nausea since yesterday afternoon. I'm done being cooped up in this room. It's time to get things done."

She sat up, eyes wide. "Like what?"

"I need to speak with Maciah first and decide the rest after. If he wants to ignore me over the fact that I saved his nest by offering up my blood, then I'm not staying here."

I wouldn't lie to myself and pretend the thought of leaving didn't hurt. I'd grown to care for these vampires over the last month of living with them. I trusted them, but I needed all of them to do the same in return. If Maciah couldn't have confidence in my choices, there was no point in letting my feelings for him continue to grow, no matter how much I wanted him while in his presence.

"You'd really leave knowing that there are plenty of people out there who want you dead?" Rachel asked, worry lacing her words.

I shrugged after buttoning my favorite jeans. "I've been killing vampires for a long time now. This is bigger than anything I've been faced with, but I know how to be careful. Plus, none of the bloodsuckers that want me dead are close now that Silas got what he wanted."

Rachel bit her lower lip and looked away from me.

"What is it?" I asked while stepping into my black boots.

"Well, we might have heard something yesterday that I didn't tell you about yet."

I finished pulling up the zippers and stalked toward her, my heels clicking on the hardwood floors as I moved. "And that would be what?"

"Maciah was going to talk to you about it," she said.

I glanced around the room, shrugging my shoulders. "Doesn't look like he's followed through on that, so why don't you?"

She sighed. "I probably should have rethought being besties with you. It's going to get me kicked out of the house again."

"Then, you can help me find a new safe house after we both leave. There really is no wrong choice to make here, Rach. Just tell me what you guys heard."

Her eyes lit up at the idea of us staying together. Even though that might have sounded exciting in the moment, I knew she'd miss this nest too much to really enjoy living with me for the long term. Rachel wasn't meant to live a life like I had before they found me.

"Okay, fine, but there are no takebacks on that promise."

I held my pinky up to indulge her. "Pinky promise."

She jumped up from the bed and squealed as her finger hooked around mine. "So, we got word from another vampire group in Europe that Dmitri is furious about his pseudo-brother being killed. Apparently, they made moves as soon as they got news of Rigo's death. They're closer than any of us realized, and he wants vengeance from the whore who killed his brother. His words, not mine obviously."

None of that surprised me. I had a feeling that would be something we'd have to deal with eventually. I just didn't think Dmitri would be acting so soon. Clearly, I'd been wrong about assuming he had more control over himself than Rigo.

"They don't know who we are, though, so we have time," I said. I'd rather be more focused on killing Silas before he became more powerful than anyone else who wanted me dead.

She sat cross-legged on the bed. "That wasn't all we heard. Someone got video of you and Maciah running to the car that picked the two of you up. They know who Maciah is. It's only a matter of time before they figure out who you are, if they haven't already."

My jaw clenched and teeth ground together. As if I didn't have enough to worry about with Silas, Viktor, and Maciah. Why not add a fourth pain-in-my-ass to the mix. It was as if I was creating my own harem of pissed-off vampires. Look at me go.

"I'm going to go talk to Maciah now," I said.

"Are you sure that's a good idea?"

My breath hitched at the thought of seeing him after almost a week apart, and her question made me hesitate, but only for a second. I needed to do this. I didn't hide from my problems. I faced them head on, even when they made my stomach feel like it was filled with concrete.

It didn't matter that I'd thought we would all work together. I couldn't count on that any longer.

The idea had been nice for the few weeks it lasted, but I should have known better. I'd allowed hope in, but I wasn't going to let the disappointment that Maciah might be just like everyone else crush me.

Nobody would ever have that power over me again.

"It's a great idea, and I'd like to do so by myself. Do you know if he's alone in his office?" I asked.

She nodded. "At least he was when I passed by on my way to see you."

Good. That was what I needed. Just me and Maciah. There was no reason to make a scene. We'd talk, and I'd make some decisions. Nothing more, nothing less.

"I'll see you after I'm done." I went to my dresser and tucked a stake into each of my boots before I left. Given that I didn't know where I stood with Maciah any longer, I was back to being paranoid about the other vampires. I wouldn't attack unless provoked, but I also wouldn't be unprepared.

I waved to Rachel as I left my room. She was still sitting on my bed, concern creasing around her eyes. I couldn't deny that I was worried as well. With every step I took down the hallway, breathing became harder and my heart beat faster than normal.

By the time I arrived at his door, my palms were sweaty, and I had to wipe them over my jeans. I thought I'd mentally prepared myself for this moment, but that obviously wasn't the case. Regardless, I was there, and I wasn't turning back.

My knuckles rapped lightly on the wooden door, and it cracked open, allowing me to view Maciah before he saw me.

He was sitting on the couch with his head in his hand, fingers tangled in his long hair. His dress shirt was untucked, and there were suit jackets and ties strewn across the cushions behind him.

Maciah's head slowly lifted, and our gazes locked as I stepped into the room, closing the door behind me. He had dark circles under his creased eyes, telling me he hadn't been properly feeding since I'd last seen him. I tried not to be happy that he looked miserable, but I couldn't deny a small part of me was glad to see I wasn't the only one affected by our time apart.

His nearly black eyes appraised me, causing chills to run over my skin. "Amersyn." His voice was low and full of heartbreak.

I wanted to go to him, to hold him and make all this hurt between us stop, but that wasn't why I was there. Maciah's absence had spoken volumes. He'd made a choice just like I had, and I needed to stay strong, no matter how out of control my emotions were getting by seeing him again. For now, I was going to blame the heightened senses I'd been experiencing the last few days.

"We need to talk," I said with an even tone.

"I was going to come see you today. I thought you weren't able to get out of bed?" he asked without getting up from the couch.

"I'm better now. Can we talk, or are you busy?" I needed to get to the point before I forgot what I'd come here for.

Maciah stood from the couch. His shoulders were slumped, and his stride was sluggish. He made it behind his desk and took a seat. His hand brushed dark strands of hair behind his ear before looking up at me. "What did you want to talk about?"

I sat across from him, steeling my resolve to remain detached with my words and reactions. I wouldn't feel bad for him. I'd been the one stuck in bed for days, the one who had almost sacrificed herself for freaking vampires.

Maciah had every opportunity to come to me if he'd been regretting his decision to walk away. Any hurt he was feeling was his own fault.

"I'd like to know what you've found out while I've been recovering," I said, leaving out the fact that Rachel had already filled me in a little bit.

"Is that all?" he asked, sounding almost hopeful.

"There isn't anything else to discuss, is there?" I asked in return.

He leaned forward, gripping the arms of his chair. "I guess not," he snapped.

Mood swings much?

He didn't get to be mad at me. I'd done nothing wrong. I wasn't going to put up with his attitude, especially not after the week of torture I'd been through.

"I came here hoping to have a civil conversation with you, but if you're still pissed at me, then maybe it's best I left," I said, hating the words as they came out of my mouth.

"How did you think I was going to feel after you almost got yourself killed?" he sneered.

"Better than having everyone die because we were severely outnumbered, but that's not why you're mad, is it?" I asked, because I wasn't sure if he even understood why he was angry.

Maciah's eyes narrowed as he crossed his arms, staying silent.

"Let me see if I can clear this up for you. The plan didn't go the way you expected and that made you upset. You tried to gain control of the situation, but Silas had us in a lose-lose spot, further infuriating the leader in you. Me, someone who is supposed to be yours to protect, ended up doing the protecting. An action that scared and confused you. Maybe you didn't know how to process those emotions, so you settled on wrath. When you didn't know who to be mad at, you chose to blame me, the one who stopped a massacre from happening in your nest. Sound about right?"

"You have no idea what you're talking about," Maciah spat through gritted teeth.

"I think I do. Except, I didn't expect this kind of reaction from you. Not for as long as you've dragged it out. I thought you had more sense. I thought you cared about me and respected me, but I was wrong."

My fury rose as I continued to speak. Time hadn't made any of this better. Maciah wasn't the leader I thought he was. I wouldn't sit here and argue with him. Not when I had more important things to worry about, like staying alive.

Some of the rage deflated out of him as his eyes lightened and he let out a soft sigh. "I still care about you, Amersyn."

I scoffed. "You have an odd way of showing it."

"You didn't listen to me. I could have figured something else out. Instead, you put yourself in danger. How did you think that was going to make me feel?" His voice rose, but he wasn't yelling. The tone was filled with anguish.

"I expected you to trust me. I'm sure you think I'm an irrational hunter who doesn't know what she's doing, but I knew the choice I was making, and it was the right one. If you can't see that by now, then I'm not sure you ever will. The only reason I'd chosen to stay here was because I thought we could be a team. I was wrong, and that changes things."

He stood and turned away from me. My throat burned with heavy emotions. This wasn't what I wanted. I wasn't sure what I expected, but I didn't like the reality.

I moved to leave. I'd been through enough suffering as of late.

As I stood, Maciah finally spoke while staring out the window. "You were right."

"Excuse me?" I turned to face him again, needing to be sure I'd heard him correctly.

"You made the right choice for the nest, but it wasn't the right one for you and I thought you were going to die. I failed to protect you, Amersyn." He twisted back toward me, eyes bright with emotions I couldn't identify.

"You might have been called to be my protector, but that doesn't only mean you're tasked with keeping me safe. It also means that you're supposed to support me, guide me, and stand by my side, even if I make a choice that you don't necessarily agree with."

When he didn't say anything, I continued.

"Keeping me safe isn't always going to be possible, and if you can't accept that, then we're done here. I won't deal with whatever is currently happening every time things don't go our way, because I guarantee you that's going to happen several times over. There are three more vampires after me. Nothing about the choices we'll have to make in the near future will be simple. I need you to trust me like you did when I killed Rigo on my own."

Maciah closed the distance between us. His steps were sure and steady. I was standing in front of the chair and looking up at him as he reached for me.

The coolness of his touch caused shivers to race down my body and cracked open the fissures that had been forming in my heart since our time apart. I'd missed him more than I'd let myself believe.

"I do trust you, and I don't want to be done with you. I don't want you to leave. I'm sorry I didn't come see you. I was ashamed and didn't want to face the hurt I'd caused by not supporting you," Maciah said, pulling me toward him.

I hesitated and kept a distance between us as I held my stance firm. I wasn't sure how I was supposed to respond to him. It was exactly what I'd wanted him to say, but I'd hoped for those words days ago.

He had made me care and then abandoned me. By the way my body and emotions still reacted to him, I knew he held a power over me that could crush my heart. I'd made myself a promise that I wouldn't ever let that happen again. Yet, even as I stood there wanting to walk away, I couldn't find the strength to pull out of his hold.

His grip tightened around my hands. "I didn't mean to hurt you."

"But you did."

"I'm more regretful of that than anything else. Can you find a way to give me a chance to fix this?" he asked, eyes darkening once again.

My first thought was to answer with no, but things weren't that simple. Maciah wasn't another hunter, and I wasn't exactly human. This was different from my past. I could admit that to myself. My feelings toward him were stronger than anything I'd experienced before.

A part of me believed that Maciah wasn't lying, that he was truly apologetic for his choices, but if I forgave him for abandoning me when I needed him most, then what did that mean for me?

I could be setting myself up for future hurt, and I wasn't about that. I'd had enough of that in my life. It was the reason I'd always kept people at a distance. I hadn't expected to worry about these emotions with vampires.

I didn't expect to care so much.

CHAPTER 2

I NEEDED MORE TIME BEFORE I COULD DECIDE IF THINGS were fixable between the two of us. I wanted them to be, but that didn't mean it was the best choice. Possibly not for either of us. Protectors weren't supposed to have feelings for the heirs, and I understood why. Whatever was between us was making the situation more complicated than it needed to be.

Removing myself from his hold, I turned toward the door without meeting Maciah's gaze. "I think we need more time apart before making any decisions."

Every step away from Maciah was harder than the last as I walked away from him. As I reached for the handle, he appeared in front of me.

His hands were hovering over me, begging to touch me, but knowing they didn't currently have the right. Our gazes locked, and I nearly stumbled back from the intensity of Maciah's dark eyes, so full of need as he stared into mine.

My core tightened as he leaned in closer. His breath warmed my cheeks, and my chest rose and fell in rapid succession as I waited for what he was going to do next. This was the Maciah I had missed. The one who had been so sure of himself. The one who made me feel safe and wanted, even when he infuriated me.

A part of me screamed to push him away. He'd left me alone. Yet, I'd missed him and his touch. The internal struggle was unlike anything I'd ever experienced.

"I can't be in this house with you any longer and not have you. I made a mistake and, even though I don't deserve your forgiveness, I'm begging for you to give me another chance," he whispered against my neck as he inhaled my scent, all while keeping his hands to himself.

I moved, and he shadowed my movements perfectly. As soon as my back was to the door, I let my head fall back against the wooden surface, then tried and failed to find the words to respond.

"I'm so damn sorry, Amersyn." He inched closer to me, lifting a hand to my face and pausing his movements as I closed my eyes.

If he touched me, I was done for. I wouldn't be

able to walk away. The me I was before meeting these vampires was screaming to get the hell out of there, but things weren't as black and white as I'd once believed. Maciah wasn't a monster. He wasn't the only one who made mistakes.

When I didn't move, he continued, "Only shame kept me away, and I need you to forgive me, to let me make this right."

The truth of his statement sent shivers down my spine, and I made the conscious choice to lean into his touch. I couldn't ignore his pleas. Maciah would get the forgiveness he asked for, but it would be the only chance. I wouldn't feel abandoned again, but I also couldn't imagine never having his lips on mine again. Keeping him at bay was not only hurting him, but myself, and I didn't want to walk away from him, wondering what might have been.

My fingers fisted around the soft material of Maciah's shirt, and I held on to him as he lifted his other hand to my face and brought his lips down to mine. I opened my mouth to him, our tongues and teeth clashing in a passionate dance that had me gripping him tighter.

"You have no idea how much I've craved you… needed you," he murmured against my lips.

My only reply was an incoherent murmur as he lifted me up and carried me to his desk.

Maciah's distance had hurt me, but there was no

denying how miserable he'd been as well. I wouldn't fight something that made my heart swell and my need unstoppable. Not when I truly believed the sincerity of his words.

I wrapped my legs around his waist as he lay me back on the smooth surface of his desk. His hands moved up my sides, lifting my sweater until the material came over my head. Goosebumps rose along my skin even as his touch left a trail of fire in its wake.

Nothing about this could be wrong.

I grabbed his face, pulling him closer to me while leaning forward to kiss him again and locking my ankles around his ass. His closeness was soothing the dark edges around me that had been resurfacing as I'd stayed holed up in my room.

Maciah's tongue swirled over my lips before tangling with my own in a way so tantalizing that I let out a stifled moan before he made his way back down my neck.

"You can't let fear keep you from me again, or I won't be so forgiving," I muttered as I arched my back and tilted my head, giving him better access.

He sucked the sensitive spot above my collarbone. "Never again. I promise."

His fingertips moved slowly over my chest, then down my sides before gripping my hips. He stared down at me with no hesitation in his eyes. "I won't ever hurt you again, Amersyn."

The words were a pledge, one I knew he meant, and I hoped he could keep no matter what obstacles came our way.

I grabbed both sides of his face, pulling him back to me. There was a lightness inside me, soothing the anxiety that had been building over the last week. Maciah was the balm to that ache. His only fault was that he cared too much. I needed him just as much as he seemed to need me.

That thought scared the hell out of me, but not in the way I expected. As his touch heated my skin, calling to me like nothing before, I knew that this was a risk in life worth taking. The feelings for him that had been there since day one were what had kept me from running away before and why I was staying now.

I wanted nothing more than to trust the bond between us and believe that everything would find a way to work itself out, as long as neither of us gave up.

My thoughts had me holding on to Maciah tighter, needing him as close as possible, but as my need ramped up, Maciah's kisses slowed.

He pulled away just a few inches as he reached for my sweater that he'd previously taken off me.

"I'm sorry," he said, grazing his knuckles down my arms.

I laughed and gestured between us. "I think it's clear there aren't any other apologies needed."

He smirked. "While I'm thankful for that, I meant for going after you the way I did. I couldn't leave things as they were and let you walk away. You make me lose control like nothing else."

I rested my hand over his chest. "I'm glad you did."

Maciah tugged the soft material of my v-neck back over my head, then kissed my forehead. "I should probably apologize for undressing you, too, but I'm not actually sorry about that and I promised I wouldn't lie to you."

My grin matched his. "I appreciate that."

"So, we're okay? Me and you?" he asked, helping me off the desk as I got control over my hormones. They wanted to move faster than I was previously comfortable with.

"We're going to be just fine as long as we learn from our mistakes," I said confidently.

"Agreed." He laced his fingers through mine, and a crease formed between his eyes. "As much as I'd like to take you back to my room, I should get you caught up on what I've learned this week. We don't know how much time we have."

"Rachel filled me in a little about the threat from

Dmitri and that there hadn't been eyes on Silas or Viktor yet," I said, hoping there wasn't much more to tell than that.

"I purposely left a few details out when Rachel was around. I didn't want her to share everything and have the information interfere with you getting better," Maciah said, sounding more like the vampire leader I first met.

"I figured as much. What else is there? Hopefully, something more about Silas," I replied. That vampire really needed to die first.

He shook his head. "Nobody can find him. He disappeared after leaving here, and unless he has underground entrances to his places in Salem and Sacramento, he didn't return to either of them."

"What do you think that means?" I asked.

"I don't know, but we'll figure it out. What we do know is that Dmitri knows exactly who you are now, and I believe we have Viktor to thank for that. We still haven't spotted him either, but we know he's left Russia. I have teams searching for all three of them. We won't leave any stone unturned until they surface."

"How do you have the resources to do all of this?" I had no problem trusting that he had everything handled if he said as much, but if we needed help, I could possibly reach out to some of the hunters I'd met throughout the years. They wouldn't mind spying and possibly killing vampires.

"Our nest isn't the only one who wants things to go back to the old ways. There are more of us out there that don't want to be feared for what they've become. They might not be capable of attacking bigger nests like Silas's, but they can be useful when it comes to keeping an eye on things."

Sounded similar to the hunters I was thinking of.

"Okay, so what's our next step?" I asked. Now that I didn't feel like death, I intended to be part of the decisions going forward.

"Dmitri is headed our way. We don't know when or how he'll make his move, but he has every intention of killing you. Twice. He knows you're the heir and what you'll become when you die, and I suspect he plans to make you suffer for killing Rigo."

I grinned. "Suffering. Sounds like my kind of guy."

Maciah grew solemn. "This isn't a joke, Amersyn. You're not hunting street scum anymore."

I gave his hand a squeeze. "I know that. Why do you think I came to you instead of just leaving when I was healed? But knowing that doesn't mean I have to live in fear."

A rumble built in his chest. "Fear can be a good thing when it comes to survival."

"Yeah, and it can also be bad, but we're going to

figure this out together and trust each other while doing so, right?"

His smooth palms rubbed up and down my arms. "You're right. We'll do this together."

Just a month ago, I didn't think I could trust anyone. Maciah had made that trust falter over the last several days, but my instincts kept pushing me toward him, and I was grateful they had. I wanted to see what happened when I put my faith in the right people instead of ones who only sought to use and control me like Caleb had when he'd rescued me from the streets.

He'd been older and more resourceful and made me promises that I'd believed without hesitation. All I'd cared about was that someone finally knew something about the monsters I'd seen and wanted to teach me how to become the hunter I needed to be.

I shuddered. No, I wouldn't think of those early days. Not when I was so close to vengeance.

Maciah lifted my chin. "Are you okay?"

My lips lifted into a smile. "Absolutely."

CHAPTER 3

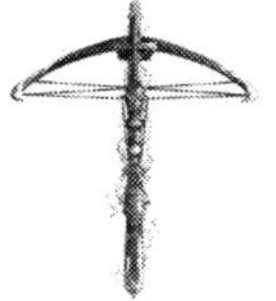

MACIAH MIGHT HAVE BEEN IN A BETTER MOOD AFTER our talk, but he was still in a bad way. We left his office and I forced him straight to the kitchen.

"You need to eat. Or drink. Or whatever," I said, pushing him toward the fridge.

"I thought I was supposed to be your protector," he muttered.

I rolled my eyes. "Now, you're being dramatic as well as stubborn. Can you even remember the last time you had blood?"

He turned to me slowly, eyes nearly black. "The day we got home from LA."

Damn him. He'd truly been torturing himself.

I kept my thoughts to myself as he grabbed a couple bags of blood and a mug. I turned to peek out the kitchen window. I might not be as grossed out by the crimson liquid as I used to be, but I still didn't want to see it sloshing into his glass.

The rose bushes were covered in frost, and everything seemed quiet outside, but that wasn't a good thing to me. Silence made me uncomfortable. I lived for movement and action. Anything that brought me closer to what I'd been fighting for all these years.

My life had been turned into chaos over the last month, but I had no regrets about the choices I'd made that brought me to this moment.

"How long can vampires go without blood?" I asked, turning around to find Maciah already had the mug to his lips.

He gulped greedily, and I immediately felt bad for asking a question, rushing his feeding. Or maybe that was how he always drank when near starving. Who knew?

Maciah pulled the cup away from his lips and walked toward me. He had a small drop of blood pooled at the corner of his mouth and my first thought was to kiss it away. I gave my head a small shake. Absolutely not. I wasn't a vampire. One day I knew I would be and my aversion to blood would have to change, but I would not crave something humans didn't need to consume in order to survive. Not freaking happening.

Maciah must have caught me staring at his

mouth, because his thumb rubbed over each corner, wiping away any evidence of what he'd been devouring.

"Depending on the vampire, we can go anywhere from a week to two weeks without feeding. After a week, our body begins to shut down slowly and dry out, starting with our organs first," Maciah said, answering my question that I'd already forgotten about.

"You were nearly at a week. You'd have let yourself starve?" I didn't want to believe he was that obstinate, but maybe I underestimated how much I meant to the vampire.

"He might have, but I wasn't going to let him," Zeke said as he waltzed into the kitchen, grinning. "It's nice to see you out of bed, Amersyn. Even better to see Maciah out of his office and done with his wallowing." He sniffed the air. "A shower might also be helpful, though."

Maciah turned to his second-in-command, leveling him with a dark sneer. "Watch what you say."

Zeke shrugged, unfazed by the powerful vampire. "You might be the leader around here, but you were making poor choices. I'm just here to make sure you don't make the same mistakes again."

Zeke had a point. Maciah hadn't been putting his nest at the forefront of his thoughts. I'd distracted him from taking care of everything he'd been building. That didn't sit well with me.

Eddie walked in next, dressed in all black as if he was just going on guard duty or getting done. He nodded at each of us, his auburn hair falling over his eyes as he did so.

"Anything new to report?" Zeke asked Eddie, becoming more serious than I usually saw him.

"Just a long night in freezing weather. Everything was quiet. Even more than normal," Eddie answered.

Huh. I'd thought the same thing when I'd been staring out the window. His comment didn't make me feel any better.

Rachel and Nikki entered the kitchen as well. It was like a beacon had been sent out and everyone wanted to be part of the party. Or it was possible they were all just hungry.

With the overcrowding, I was getting uncomfortable and ready to leave. I sidestepped Maciah only to have Rachel and Nikki block me in.

"You didn't come see me when you were done," Rachel said with crossed arms and disappointment. She'd gotten too used to having me all to herself while I was stuck in bed.

"Who said I was done?" I asked with a raised brow.

Her fingers drummed over her biceps. "True. Is everything back to normal now?"

I grinned. She wasn't the best at subtlety.

Maciah swooped in, towering over all three of us. "You don't need to be privy to everything that happens between the two of us."

Rachel's eyes narrowed on Maciah, but before she could say anything, I saved the moment from escalating. I stepped between them, keeping one hand gripping Maciah's waist while facing my friends. "Everything is fine. I'm all healed up. Everyone is on the same page. Now, we need to find at least one of the three psychos looking for me before I lose my mind."

"Amen, Amersyn. We need some action around here," Zeke said from the other side of the kitchen.

"No. We need resolution with the least amount of risk," Maciah said gruffly.

Nikki nodded. "Maciah's right. Now that we're all one big happy family again, we should probably decide our next move carefully. The only way to keep any risk low is to be in control of the situation we're walking into."

"I agree," I said, partly because she was right and partly because I was ready to turn more vampires to ash. The less of them I hunted, the more innocents that got hurt. Plus, I was more than eager for the target to be removed from my back, so I could get back to doing what I enjoyed.

Though I knew that wouldn't look the same as it

did before, I'd find a way to make it work somehow. I had to for my own sanity.

Eddie stood behind our little group, completely out of place and awkward. I nodded toward him. "What do you think?"

His eyes widened as he glanced behind himself. "Me?"

"Yep. You." He was one of the main guards and likely knew things, maybe even stuff that didn't always get passed along to those in charge. Plus, an outside opinion never hurts.

"I…um…well…" Eddie glanced at Zeke then Maciah. "I think we're doing everything we can with the information we have."

"Not the answer I was looking for, Eddie. Pretend these two imposing vampires aren't here. If you were in charge, what would you do?"

He met my eyes, staying focused only on me as he answered and seeming surer of himself when he wasn't stopped. "Considering how hard everyone has been working and all that has happened in the last week, I'd step away from the situation. Take a day off and come back with a fresh mind to see how things look after some separation and relaxation."

I cocked my head to the side. That was more insightful than I'd expected. He was right. I could see the wear on everyone. Even Rachel, who was always positive, had snapped at me.

"Thank you, Eddie. We're going to take your advice," I said, and he gulped before making a quick exit.

"What do you mean?" Rachel asked.

"We need a break. Between training, killing, researching, and healing, have any of us taken a moment to not think about the vampires who want me dead? Even when I was on my own, I took breaks by training other humans. It was a way to remove myself from being a hunter and feel normal. I know that *normal* is a relative term now, but I think it will be helpful."

"We could go to the club to let loose," Nikki suggested.

"Absolutely not," Maciah snapped, unsurprisingly, then softened. "But Amersyn is right. We'll take the rest of the day off."

"Together, or separate?" Zeke asked.

I said, "Together" at the same time Maciah said, "Separate."

"We'll let the two of you sort that out. Just let us know what the plan is once you do," Nikki said, pulling Rachel back.

I shook my head. "How about we split the day? It's still early. We could do something together now, have dinner and then take the evening to ourselves."

Maciah took my hand. "What do you suggest we do together?"

"How about watching a movie or two?" I wasn't normally a fan of doing nothing, but maybe dumbing down our thoughts with fiction would be helpful in some twisted way. And it kept us on the property, which I knew would make Maciah happy.

"I can make popcorn," Rachel said with a grin.

Zeke groaned. "Keep that crap away from me. The kernels always irritate my fangs."

She sighed. "I didn't say you had to eat it, but what's a movie day without popcorn?"

"You could always use it to throw at people," I suggested, garnering a glare from Rachel and smirks from Nikki and Zeke.

I glanced up at Maciah. "What do you think?" If we were going to be working together, he had to be okay with this break as well.

"I think as long as I get you to myself tonight, then I don't care what we do today," he answered quietly while the others chatted about movies to pick.

"That shouldn't be a problem," I replied, and my anxiety at being alone with Maciah after nearly a week apart spiked. Not normal unease, just more complicated feelings. I'd told myself I'd take things slowly with him, but my hormones thought a month was plenty slow.

If I was willing to forgive Maciah so completely, I shouldn't be nervous about having sex with him. Except something told me that sex with Maciah wouldn't be like anything I'd experienced in my past. There was something deeper between us, and, if we took this step, there was no going back.

I'd be all in with the vampires. I'd have crossed a line I never thought possible.

The hunter in me was still fighting against that possibility, but if I was going to stand a chance at staying alive and getting the justice I sought, I needed to move past all my previous reservations.

I deserved that and so did Maciah.

WE ENDED UP WATCHING THREE MOVIES, HAVING several food fights, and completely wrecked the media room, but the mess we'd have to clean up later was worth the smiles on everyone's faces. Even Maciah's.

There was a snack bar in the media room that had been mostly stocked with blood but had been emptied by the time we were done. Maciah had a glow about him when we exited the room that I didn't think I'd ever seen on the vampire leader.

I'd also eaten all of the human food that I could before it had been thrown at others, so I was feeling more like a stuffed pig and not at all hungry for the dinner we'd talked about earlier.

"What now?" Rachel asked, pulling popcorn from her long dark strands.

"Now, I'm going to fall into a food coma," I said.

Zeke haphazardly high-fived me. "Agreed."

"I'm going to go shower. Probably twice just to get the ketchup out of my hair," Nikki groaned, but there was an obvious grin on her face as she spoke.

Rachel frowned. "So, that's it? Fun time is over?"

I nudged her. "That doesn't mean it won't ever happen again. We can have a girl's night soon, too."

Oh, how things had changed. I was comforting a vampire with promises of more hang-out time. I wanted to be disappointed or annoyed, but instead, I was content. The day had been spent just how we all needed.

"I need to go check in with the guards on duty before I settle in. If you're not ready to go back to your room, you can join me," Zeke offered Rachel.

She seemed hesitant to accept his offer, but finally nodded her head. "Sure."

The two of them ventured off, and Nikki said her goodbyes as well. When it was just Maciah and me in the hallway, he pressed me against the wall. "Your room or mine?"

As much as I didn't want to go back to being stuck in my room, I wanted to change and possibly shower after the food fights. "Mine if you don't mind."

"As long as you don't mind me staying," he said.

"I suspected as much. We can stop by your room first if you need anything," I offered.

He scooped me up. "I have everything I need right here."

Maciah was an expert at swoony comments. So much so that I wondered if he'd had any practice in the past. He'd lived nearly eight decades. There had to have been other women, but instead of asking about them, I decided it was none of my business. What was in the past needed to stay there.

As he walked with me in his arms toward my room, I rested my head against his chest. His skin wasn't icy, but it was noticeably cooler than mine, just like all other vampires. For the first time, though, the temperature difference didn't bother me.

"I probably won't be there when you wake up. I have a couple of calls with other nests scheduled at weird times since some of them are international," Maciah said as we entered my room.

I wiggled out of his grasp. "Anything you'll want help with?"

"No, but if anything comes from the conversations, I'll get you up. I promise," he said.

I headed into the bathroom next and took one look in the mirror before turning on the shower. I had chip crumbs, ketchup, and popcorn in places they didn't belong.

"I'll just be five minutes," I called to Maciah before shutting the door.

He was already on my bed, taking off his shoes. "Take your time."

Right. Like that was going to happen.

The door clicked closed and I was undressed in seconds before stepping under the hot water. The day had gone better than I ever could have expected. Everything felt like it was back on track, even though we'd learned nothing new. Taking time to be ourselves was the solution we hadn't been looking for.

Once the crap was out of my hair, I stepped out of the shower and reached for my towel, realizing that I'd forgotten to grab new clothes. I could awkwardly put my dirty ones back on, or I could be a grown-ass woman and walk out in my towel.

Stupid hormones were the cause of my hesitancy, but I didn't let that last for long. Instead, I opted for ignoring Maciah completely once I opened the bathroom door, and I took swift steps toward my closet, quietly shutting the sliding door with a racing heart. I could hear Maciah's chuckle through the wood and flipped him off even though he couldn't see me. I knew I was being ridiculous. He'd already seen me naked, but that was before I was tempted to sleep with him. Things were different now.

Instead of continuing to stress, I focused on

getting dressed. My hair was soaking my back, so I flipped my head down and wrapped my towel around the wet strands before grabbing underwear and a long shirt.

After getting clothed, I checked my hair again, wringing it out once more before putting it into a braid, and opening the closet door.

Maciah was in my bed, half under the covers and without a shirt. I also noticed his dress pants were on the floor next to his shoes at the foot of my bed. Yeah, there was a sexy vampire in my bed wearing only boxer briefs and I wasn't going to try to sleep with him.

I was internally laughing at myself while simultaneously crying.

"Feel better?" Maciah asked.

I crawled into bed, trying to ignore my inner struggle. "Much. You?"

He wrapped his arms around me, tucking me into his side. "From this morning? Yes. You made the right call today."

"I'm glad you can agree that I'm the superior decision-maker here," I joked.

He squeezed around my ribs. "Not exactly what I meant by that."

"Close enough." My heart was pounding rapidly from his closeness, and I clenched my legs together as I tried to turn over and give Maciah my back.

He grabbed my shoulder, pulling me back toward him. "You don't have to be nervous. I'll never expect something from you that you're not ready for, Amersyn."

I almost told him he had no idea what he was talking about, but then I remembered he could probably smell the damn sexual tension and I wanted to bury myself under the blankets. Except I didn't hide from my problems.

"Good, because I don't have a problem telling you no," I said, then turned over again.

This time he didn't stop me. Instead, he decided to torture me by dragging his fingertips lightly over my heated skin, tracing over my tattoo until I was nearly a quivering mess beneath his touch.

"Maciah…"

"Yes, Amersyn?"

I rolled over to face him, wishing he had a shirt on so I could grip the fabric and pull him closer. "Kiss me."

Without responding, Maciah's lips were on mine, and he was suddenly on top of me, our bodies aligned and pressed together, closer than they'd ever been.

My hands roamed over his exposed skin, grabbing his ass and pulling him tighter to me. His hardened length twitched between my legs, begging for attention, but I wasn't ready. As much as I wanted all of Maciah physically, I knew I had a mental obstacle—or two—to overcome before I could claim him.

For the time being, I accepted the foreplay he was offering and chose to enjoy the buildup we were creating. It would be worth the wait once I was ready. Or maybe I'd be smacking myself for waiting.

As Maciah's fingers moved south and my back arched, need driving me closer to him, I knew it would more than likely be the latter.

CHAPTER 4

THE FOLLOWING MORNING, I WOKE UP IN MY ROOM WITH a note from Maciah. He'd left to go make the international phone calls he'd mentioned the night before. He told me to come find him when I woke up, but after the group hang-out the day before, I was ready for some alone time before we dove back into vampire hunting.

I hadn't been outside since we got back from Los Angeles, and my muscles were feeling twitchy from the lack of exercise. Getting out of bed, I went to my closet and dressed in fleece-lined running pants, a tank top, then a sweatshirt, followed by a beanie and running shoes.

Damn, I couldn't wait for spring.

I passed the dresser with my stakes in the top drawer. I shouldn't need one, but it was always when you didn't have protection that you needed it most. So instead of overthinking, I grabbed one small stake and tucked it into the pocket on my waistband that was supposed to be for a phone. The weapon fit perfectly against my spine and wasn't noticeable, especially with my sweatshirt pulled down.

As soon as I was ready for a jog, I headed downstairs. It was early, and not many people were around as I made my way outside. Maciah's property was big enough that I could run the perimeter while breathing in fresh air without putting myself in harm's way.

I stretched, annoyed at the tension in my body. Before vampires were continually hunting me, I was active every day in some form or another. Perks of living above a gym and killing bloodsuckers most nights.

My breath came out in puffs of fog in front of me as I began to jog toward the fence line. I figured if I followed that, nobody would be threatened by me being near the cabins. It wasn't like they didn't all know who I was by then.

With every stride, my pulse quickened, and the buzz of the workout filled me. The birds that hadn't migrated south were just waking, and I smiled as they chirped when I passed through the trees.

Making things right with Maciah was exactly what I needed to feel ready about facing these other vampires. I'd get my core strength back up to where it needed to be, and then we'd go hunting. There would be no sitting around waiting for vampires to appear. That wasn't how I got things done before, and it wouldn't be how I did them now.

Hopefully, Maciah would agree with me. I wanted to be done fighting with him. I wanted us to be equal partners and have him trust me like he'd done in LA when I'd gone after Rigo. If we could stay like that, then I'd know I made the right decision to stay and forgive him.

The edge of the property was coming up. I'd never been this far back before, and I was surprised to see that the fence ended, but there was a vampire standing at the corner. A black ball cap sat low over his eyes, and he wore the black tactical clothing that I was used to seeing the guards wear along with some sort of ski mask, half covering his face, and likely keeping out the cold.

I nodded at him as I passed, and he returned the gesture as I hurried along. It was too early in the morning to strike up a conversation with a vampire I'd never met. Based on what little I could see of his face, I didn't believe I'd met him before.

At the next corner, there was another guard stationed, dressed the same as the prior one and keeping watch.

With another bob of my head, I continued my

way around the property, increasing my pace as I neared the mansion. I thought I'd be tiring easier after so many days in bed, but I went another lap without hesitation.

The sun was rising higher in the sky, and I was thankful for the slight warmth its rays provided as my feet continued to pound against the earth.

Three laps seemed like a good number. After that, I could head to the gym and do some sparring with whoever was present and not afraid to get too close to me. It wasn't often vampires were willing to practice with someone who once wanted them dead. Though, I could always count on Rachel or Nikki to join me.

My steps slowed as I realized the first guard at the fence line was missing on my third time around. I checked behind me and then toward the other end, and I couldn't see the second one, either. I listened for sounds, but there was nothing. Not even the birds I'd heard earlier.

The wind began to pick up, and so did my senses. I didn't like the empty feeling in my chest. I walked quietly forward and considered cutting through the cabin area to get back to the mansion quicker or to find another guard I was familiar with, like Eddie.

Brush rustled behind me, and I whirled around to find three vampires, all dressed like Maciah's guards, but their eyes were crimson instead of muddy-red.

"Good morning, boys. Is there something I can help you with?" I asked, acting as if I was unaware that they didn't belong. I only had the one stake on me, which would do me no good against three vampires, so I left it tucked away for the moment, hoping there was a small chance these bloodsuckers didn't want to kill me.

None of them said anything as they spread out, getting nearer. I wasn't going to be able to talk myself out of this one.

I turned and began to run toward the mansion while reaching for the stake. I hated feeling like a coward, but I also wasn't fond of dying. I was going to need more help if I could find it.

Before I'd made it even ten feet or was able to pull out my only weapon, another vampire dropped from the trees right in front of me. "Going somewhere, Amersyn?"

The cropped blond hair, crooked nose, and thin lips were features I'd never forget.

"Dmitri," I spat, dropping my arms. Something told me that it was better to keep the stake hidden until I was up close and personal with the bloodsucker.

"I wondered if you'd remember me," he said with a Russian accent even more pronounced than Rigo's had been.

I narrowed my eyes at him. "I'd never forget the monsters who—"

Something hard slammed into the side of my head, and I crashed onto the ground. Dmitri was on top of me before I could process what had happened.

"We're going to go have a little chat. Except I'll be the only one doing the talking," he sneered, grabbing hold of my neck and squeezing.

I brought both of my knees up, ramming them into the back of his thighs. He fell forward, but that only made him press down harder on my throat.

Twisting beneath him, I did everything I could to get out from under his weight, but the other vampires moved in, grabbing my arms and legs, making it impossible to reach for my stake.

"Let's make this easier on all of us," Dmitri said right before he punched the side of my head, knocking me right the hell out.

WHEN I WOKE UP, I WAS IN A DARK ROOM WITH NO windows or lights on, but I already knew I wasn't alone. The smell of decaying flesh hit me as soon as I came to, and I began to tug on the abrasive ropes on my wrists.

"Going somewhere?" Dmitri's voice echoed through the small space.

"Nope. Just getting comfortable," I replied.

He clicked on a light from across the room, causing me to squint from the change. Concrete walls surrounded us and there were no windows, so I assumed we were underground somewhere. There was no way to know how long I'd been unconscious, and I had no clue where I was. Hell, I could have been in Russia for all I knew.

Dmitri stalked forward and backhanded me without notice. Blood pooled inside my mouth from his force and coated the inside of my mouth as my jaw rattled. Crap, that had hurt.

"Don't get smart with me, girl. I have no problem gagging you, no matter how much I'm looking forward to hearing your screams while we get to know each other," Dmitri said.

Behind him, there was a table of metal torture devices glinting under the lamp he'd turned on.

"I can't wait," I deadpanned, then spat my blood onto the floor next to his shiny black shoes.

He gripped my chin between his thumb and forefinger. "You don't have a sensible bone in your body if you're not terrified of me."

"What is the point of fear if I've already accepted that I'm going to die?" I asked. This monster wasn't going to get the thrills he was seeking from me. I wouldn't allow him one enjoyable moment of killing me.

Dmitri's fist made an introduction to my cheek, and my chair tilted far enough back that I landed on the floor, still tied to the stupid seat. My hands burned in agony at being crunched between the hard ground and metal chair. My wrist was turned at an uncomfortable angle, and I nearly cried from the shooting pains racing up my arms, but instead, I focused on one positive.

The idiot hadn't searched me after he'd knocked me out back at Maciah's nest.

The metal tip of my stake was poking through my pants and into my pinky. The slightest hope filled me that I just might have a real chance at getting out of this room alive.

Dmitri yanked me back up by my hair, taking a handful of ebony strands with him when he released me. "You've pissed a lot of people off, Amersyn. You could have stayed under the radar forever and none of us would have been the wiser, but you couldn't do that, could you? I'd told Viktor that the rumors of Darius's heir were false after we found your family. Your brother had been too weak to be anything special."

I snarled at his words, leaning forward, but not at all intimidating him with my pathetic movements.

"We never suspected you could be who we sought. An unworthy female." His lip raised in disgust at my existence, as if his was so much more worthy.

The vampire put a glove on his right hand and picked up a scalpel, twirling it between his fingers. "I'm supposed to bring you to Viktor. He doesn't like to get his hands dirty nowadays, but he is nothing to me. Not anymore. So I'll be taking the credit for your death myself."

A scream tore from my lips as he stabbed just beneath my collarbone with the small blade, hitting bone as he twisted the metal around, shredding the muscles in that area. "Does it burn like Rigo did when you stabbed him?"

"Your brother was a dirty parasite who deserved exactly what he got," I snapped in reply through clenched teeth.

Dmitri jerked the scalpel from my chest and slammed it into my leg next. "Just like you're going to. I wonder how many veins I can destroy before you bleed out."

It seemed like everyone wanted to drain me of my blood. Lucky me.

Unfortunately for Dmitri, I wasn't ready to die.

My fingers painfully fisted together as I focused only on the ropes at my wrists. If I could stand and get my one stake free, then I could turn Dmitri to ash before he had a chance to kill me even once.

He left the scalpel buried in my thigh and turned

around to find something else to torment me with. I used that distraction to jerk harder on the ropes. If I didn't hurry, I'd lose too much blood and my strength with it.

I calmed my mind and focused on the things I knew to be true. I wasn't dead, and I didn't have to be. I was technically a vampire in a human body with enhanced abilities. The ropes around my wrists and ankles couldn't hold me. I was stronger than anything in this room.

Closing my eyes, I ignored the burning pain in my right leg and the blood flowing down my chest. I only paid attention to the swift movements of my hands and the fact that the rope was getting looser.

"Have you ever been collared?" Dmitri asked me with a hint of excitement in his voice.

I didn't bother to answer him. I just needed another minute to get free.

Before I could finish my task, he pushed my head up and wrapped a leather strap around my neck that had a double-sided wrench-looking object attached to it. Except where a wrench would be rounded, the metal on this tool was sharpened to deadly points and swiveled around close to my face as he buckled the collar. I wanted to flail and make things harder for the vampire, but getting stabbed in the eye by the contraption didn't sound like fun.

Dmitri jerked my head back, then positioned the object so that the prongs of each side dug first into my sternum, then underneath my chin, forcing me to keep my head tilted back and stare at the ceiling. Even though I tried to stay still, my continued breathing had the sharp ends biting painfully into my skin.

"Do I have your attention now?" he sneered, looming over me.

I blinked slowly, then spoke through gritted teeth to avoid moving my jaw. "I'm rather tired."

He backhanded me again. The torture wrench tore through my skin, digging mostly into my chest just above my sternum, causing more blood to drip from my body.

Dmitri removed the metal from my chin, letting it rest against my cheek while it still protruded painfully from my chest.

He ran his hand under my chin, brushing over the exposed wound, then licked the blood from his fingers. "You do taste lovely. Too bad I don't want this to end for you anytime soon and I don't have any reason to take the original power inside you. I happened to like the life I built in Russia with my brother. That is, before you came and interfered."

Ignoring his comment about my tasty blood and original power, I focused on being grateful I could move my head again, which meant I didn't have to worry about further injuring myself while trying to get free.

Dmitri went back to his selection of pain-inducing items that he'd brought with him, and I refocused on my ropes. I already felt my muscles tiring, but I wasn't going to give up. I would get free. I had no other options left.

"Hmm, I wonder how quickly this would puncture a lung?" the sick bastard pondered out loud with his back still to me.

Blood trickled down my fingers from the rope cutting into my skin as I moved my arms faster, jerking them every which way I could get them to go without making too much noise.

Thankfully, Dmitri seemed as twisted as they came. He was completely enthralled with the torture devices he had laid out.

Just as I got one hand free of the rope, he turned around with a miniature bear trap in each hand. "Care to wager how many toes you'll lose when I clamp these down on your feet?" he asked with glee.

I whimpered and turned my head away from him as I reached for the stake at my back. The slats on the back of the chair weren't wide, making my task harder than I liked, but I'd gotten this far. I wouldn't fail now.

Dmitri stood over me, and I pretended to cower beneath him, trying to fill the disgusting bloodsucker with the power he clearly sought. He grabbed a handful of hair at the base of my neck, forcing my head back. I let out a soft cry and he smirked. "That's right. You are nothing but a weak woman. I own you now, Amersyn."

With the stake finally in my hand, I narrowed my eyes at him. "Nobody owns me."

I brought the weapon forward, burying it into his chest directly over his heart and hitting my mark perfectly.

His eyes widened and mouth opened as he snarled at me with elongated fangs headed toward my already exposed neck. "If I die, so do you."

A laugh started to grow within me as I used my thumb to press the six-inch stake further inside the vampire. "I don't think so," I replied, but my words came too soon. It wasn't going to be me who got the last laugh.

Dmitri used the last of his will to rip the leather collar off me, then sank his fangs into my neck, ripping out a significant chunk of my skin and destroying a couple of my arteries while he was at it.

I gargled as Dmitri and I released each other at the same time, then I pressed my hand over the gaping wound. There was no chance of it closing before I was dead.

No, this couldn't be happening. I wasn't ready to be a vampire yet.

As I crumpled to the dirty concrete floor, Dmitri's body shriveled up next to me, but not before I caught the smirk on his face as he turned into a pile of ash that my blood began to mix with. He'd gotten part of what he wanted. Maybe he had even hoped to die. I'd never know.

A heaviness settled over me as my body began to painfully shut down. I had no idea what was going to happen next, but I had a feeling it wasn't going to be the most pleasant experience I'd ever had.

Not by a long shot.

CHAPTER 5

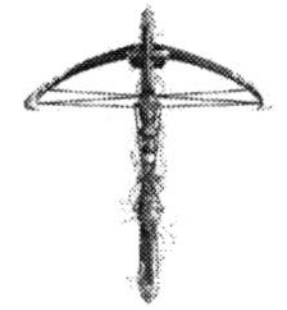

I HAD EXPECTED CONSCIOUSNESS TO FADE AWAY. IN FACT, I had hoped for that, but life had a tendency of doing the opposite of what people wanted.

My right hand stayed pressed to my neck for as long as I had the strength to do so. Blood seeped through my fingers as I tried not to breathe more than necessary. My other hand pulled the scalpel from my thigh that was still burning my skin from its metal makeup. I attempted to staunch both wounds, but I was pretty sure my femoral artery had been damaged, and not even a doctor could have helped with my neck.

Succumbing to the fact that I was going to die, I tried really hard to be thankful I wouldn't actually be dead. At least, not for long. Though, it wasn't easy to be grateful I was moments from being a vampire.

My pulse slowed, and the blood inside me began to burn inside my veins. My body became heavy as I curled into a ball, trying to keep my screams to a minimum. I had no idea where I was or how many other vampires might have been around. I wouldn't stand a chance if someone walked in while I was transforming.

Breathing was no longer possible, and panic set in. I was dying. Holy hell.

My hands clawed at my chest until they fell limp at my sides. Everything was shutting down on me except my pain receptors. Or maybe the terror was all inside my head. Either way, I was not okay.

I couldn't focus. My lungs no longer worked. Every part of me burned with a fire that I could not extinguish.

Would there ever be relief? I had major doubts there would be.

My muscles seized, forcing my body to straighten out on the bloodied floor and my back to arch up. My jaw clenched as the inferno erupted in my jawline. I couldn't stop the screech that left me. I was convinced that I would be the next one turning to ash.

The firestorm began to lessen, but I still couldn't breathe, and my inner dread was nowhere near settled. I ached to move, to take in air, to feel anything other than agony.

My prayers went unanswered as the blaze reignited inside me, moving to my neck. I did everything I could to try to move my arms and feel what was happening, but my body wasn't responding to my demands.

Tears built in my eyes and leaked down the sides of my head, falling into my hair. When the flare of fire continued to burn through me, I wished for death. A real and final death. My vengeance no longer mattered. Whatever was happening to me couldn't have been normal. Something was wrong, and I just wanted the torture to stop.

Minutes, or maybe hours, passed as I lay there, lost in the blindness of pain. The flames showed no mercy as they continued to ravage my insides. I couldn't remember anything good before this moment, nor could I fathom anything remarkable in my future.

My back arched off the ground again when it seemed as if someone had punched my solar plexus. I sucked in a breath, my eyes widening as I began to cough so harshly that I choked on air.

Wait. I could breathe. Well, sort of.

I rolled to my side and pressed my hands underneath me as I slowly got to my knees. There was so much blood around me.

My mouth salivated at its crimson color, and I

licked my lips. My gums ached and sharp points poked at my lips. Blood…sweet, delicious blood.

Oh, no. This couldn't be happening.

My fingers wrapped around my neck as the burn returned, but not because of pain.

I was hungry. Ravenous even.

My wounds were healed. I couldn't even feel scars around my neck where I knew they should have been. I tried to focus on that instead of the insatiable thirst trying to control my thoughts.

Without conscious action, my hand reached for my own blood, but I jerked my arm back before my fingertips could dip into the crimson pool before me.

"Under no circumstances am I tasting my own blood. Absolutely not," I said to myself with a solid shake of my head.

I had to get out of this room, but then I worried if I'd be able to control myself around the outside world. I didn't know where I was. I didn't know who I might hurt. Not even my growing desire to feed could convince me that becoming a murdering vampire was a good idea.

There were only two choices I could see: stay in this room and die without drinking blood, or leave with the hope that I was stronger than my thirst—that I wouldn't harm innocent humans.

As I eyed the door next to me, I knew what I had

to do. I'd never once in my life given up. I wasn't about to do so now.

With cautious steps, I turned the handle. The door creaked open, and I waited, listening for any sounds.

The hum of a motor sounded first, followed by the beating of a heart that I knew was pumping exactly what I craved.

I slammed the door shut. "No!"

My hands fisted in my hair. I had no idea how I was going to get out of this.

Taking a few deep breaths, I tried again. I couldn't stop trying. There had to be a way to find Maciah and drink the blood they had in the mansion. Food that was donated, not something I had to kill for.

I shuddered at the thought before I opened the door a second time, and instead of focusing on my surroundings, I did the opposite. I fixated on where I wanted to be: out of this building and back with Maciah.

There was a hallway in front of me, and I began to run. This would work. As long as I didn't search out the things around me, then I knew I could get back to Maciah and the others.

That was only until I forgot my speed was no longer the same as before and crashed into a wall when I was unable to slow down and turn the corner.

I was suddenly glad that I was alone. Nobody

else needed to see what a hot mess I was as a newborn.

I glanced around, double-checking that there was no one lurking in the shadows without allowing myself to concentrate too hard. If I smelled a human, I wasn't sure what I would do, and I didn't want to find out.

A streetlight shone through a window, catching my attention. It was nighttime. Mother effer. I'd been gone all day. Maybe longer than that. Maciah had to be frantic.

I used that thought to motivate me. I would figure this out. Putting one foot in front of the other, I focused on controlling my speed while taking notice of the building I had to get out of.

Stairs were up ahead. My speed picked up again as I got closer to the door. I busted through that, the metal bending against my body before slamming against the wall.

I paused to find the direction I needed to be headed only to see a group of vampires staring at me with shocked faces.

Damn it. I wasn't in the right state of mind to kill them. Or maybe I was, but for the wrong reasons.

There was a door behind the group. I had to get outside.

I sped ahead, intent to crash through the door like

I'd done to the previous one. Except these bloodsuckers had other ideas.

One of them wrapped his arms around my waist as I tried to blur by, bringing us to the ground. "Where is Dmitri?" he demanded with a Russian accent. I really hoped I wasn't in Russia.

"In hell," I muttered as I got to my knees and jerked my head back, trying to smash mine into his, but missed. The vampire had my back, and I donkey-kicked him right in the groin. His hold on me broke as he went flying a good twenty feet away from me. *Thank you, new vampire strength.*

Two others jumped in as I stood. I grabbed the first one by the neck, my nails digging into his hardened skin, causing blood to trickle out.

I took a deep inhale. No longer did these bloodsuckers smell like death. They smelled like dinner.

I had no idea if vampires ever drank from each other, but I was damn tempted as my need for food rose to the top of my priorities. Just one little bite to quench my thirst. That was all I needed.

My dark thoughts were tempting. It would be nothing to tear this vampire's neck apart using my new body.

Instead, I crushed his windpipe and threw him off me with a guttural roar of frustration. As badly as I wanted blood, I knew if I bit someone—vampire or not—then I'd find a way to justify doing so again. That wouldn't be me. Not ever.

The second one grabbed my hair before I turned around to face him. He tried to take me to the ground, but I bent over, shoved my shoulder into his stomach, and hooked my arms behind his legs before I slammed him onto the floor. As he struggled to move, I reached down and ripped his head from his body without the slightest hesitation.

Well, that was one way to take out my frustrations.

When I turned around, there were no other vampires waiting for me. I wasn't sure where they went, and I didn't care. The door leading toward the outside world held my attention as soon as I was alone.

I stepped outside, held my breath, and paused. I didn't recognize where I was. There were tall buildings, lots of lights, and too much traffic. Making my way to the street ahead, I ducked into an alley as I considered how I looked. My sweatshirt had blood covering it, along with multiple tears, and there was a hole in my pants where I'd been stabbed in the thigh. Luckily, the black concealed any of the gore that had been left behind from my previous injuries.

I took the sweatshirt off, throwing it into the shadows behind me. I was left in a tank top and my running pants and should have been freezing *if* I was still in Portland.

Or maybe it was my new vampire temperature. None of the others were ever bothered by the elements.

I could still be close to home.

My appearance was as good as it was going to get, so I stepped back into the street, looking up for something familiar.

"Mother effer," I muttered. The street sign read *S Central Ave* and there was another sign directing people to South Park.

I didn't know much about Los Angeles, but I knew of South Park. I could make my way to Maciah's other safehouse, but then I considered the night club we'd been to. Zeke knew the bouncer, Gregory. That was closer to where I was. They'd have blood and a phone. I wasn't so sure Maciah's house would have the latter.

With my destination set, I began to run, becoming a blur that the humans didn't notice as they were too engrossed in themselves. Using my new senses, I sought out other vampires. I didn't know how I could do this, but the instinct was there, like a tracking beacon leading me home. Except these bloodsuckers weren't who I really wanted.

As the street blocks passed by, I used my advanced abilities, trying to figure out what would be of most use to me. The hearing was annoying. If I tried too hard, the noises intertwined, creating nothing more than white noise inside my head.

My enhanced vision was my favorite part. I was racing over the sidewalks with speeds that had to be over two-hundred miles-per-hour. Yet, I could see every speck in the air, every bend in the road, and every person I was trying to avoid with perfect precision.

Finally, the lights to Warlock came into view. I slowed my pace, stopping in the shadows to see who was working at the front door.

I sagged in defeat when I didn't see the bald bouncer I'd met before and headed for the back side of the bar.

I had no idea who I could possibly trust. There were people after me, and I had nothing to disguise myself. Though, I looked nothing like I did the last time I'd arrived at the nightclub.

My hands rubbed over my face as I leaned against the wall. I tried to calm my emotions, but that only lasted until I sensed someone coming up behind me. I pressed myself further into the shadows and waited quietly like a beast did for their helpless prey.

Human. Blood. Thirst.

My hands wrapped around my throat, nails digging into my own skin.

I would not drink from a human.

Except as the warm body got closer, I was losing my grip on reality. The steady pulse beating from inside the human echoed through my head, calling to me like nothing else I'd ever known.

A sweet scent that would only make me feel better coated my tongue, making me salivate. It could just be one taste. Nobody would ever have to know what I did.

My hands reached out to grab the innocent being. I latched onto his shoulders, spinning him toward me, and my fangs extended to killer points, eager to take what I so desired.

Oh, God. There was a brief flicker of reality that broke through the bloodlust, but I couldn't stop my actions, no matter how I tried. The part of me that yearned for the crimson pumping inside this human was too strong.

I was going to be exactly what I hated most in this world. I was going to be a murdering vampire.

My head slowly leaned forward, the human fighting beneath my hold only fueling my excitement as I tightened my grip on him while refusing to focus on any defining features. He was nothing more than a meal. I couldn't think of this as anything else.

When my tongue swept lightly over the decadent flesh, preparing the perfect spot for my fangs to sink into, a jolt rocketed through me, painful and powerful. I dropped the human, bending to my knees with a hiss and searching for the threat.

A woman with teal hair had her hands pointed at me, but she was looking at the human I'd nearly killed. "You okay over there, Gregory?"

"I am now. Thanks, Lucy." The bouncer I'd been searching for looked closer at me. "Amersyn?"

"You know this bloodsucker?" Lucy asked as a man moved to her side, ready to attack as well.

"Sort of. What happened to you?" he asked me as I stayed perfectly still, worried one movement would have these fae striking at me again. Fae. I had no idea how I knew that's what they were, but I was sure of it from their tangy scent.

"Dmitri," I said through clenched teeth, holding my breath and unable to tear my gaze away from the veins pulsing in his neck.

"When did you turn?" he asked.

The other man stepped forward. "If she's a friend, why don't you go get her some blood before you ask any more questions?"

A blaze ignited within me as I twitched with the mention of what I needed most.

Gregory didn't respond before taking off for the club entrance. The woman was still considering me a threat, as she should. I could feel her power vibrating around us, ready to take me out at a moment's notice, but the man with her stepped closer.

"What happened to you?" he asked calmly.

"Oh, Finnigan, don't be nice to the vampire just because she's a girl," Lucy drawled.

I sneered at her, but Finnigan snapped his fingers in my face, getting my attention again. "Don't mind Lucinda. She's like that with everyone. My name is Finn. Yours is Amersyn, right?" I nodded, taking note that he seemed to prefer Finn instead of Finnigan. "Do you have anyone we can call?" he asked.

"I already took care of that," Gregory said as he raced back with a large Styrofoam cup in hand.

The brave bouncer grabbed on to my arm, dragging me further away from the club and past the two fae. "You can't be here."

"I know that, but I didn't know where else to go. I need…" I eyed the cup, wanting badly to tear it from his grasp, but somehow restrained since he seemed to be trying to help me.

"Take my keys and wait in the truck while you drink this." Gregory handed me the blood, and my gums began to burn again as I held on to it tightly. "I'm supposed to be starting my shift right now, but I'll let them know I forgot something at home and that I'll be back in a while. My truck is the white Chevy."

"What about them?" I nodded to the fae.

"You don't want anything to do with them," he said.

Lucy scoffed. "I heard that. You must not have gotten the good news. I'm a new and improved version of my prior self."

There was a grin on her face that told me that wasn't necessarily the truth, and Gregory didn't seem to believe it either.

"I told Maciah you were here, and he's already on his way. I mentioned I could ask the fae to take you home, but he'd rather come get you personally. So, I'll take you to his house down here for you to wait," Gregory said. The tension lifted from my chest, knowing Maciah was coming.

"Thank you, Gregory." Tears threatened to fall down my face. What the hell was wrong with me? I knew I was relieved, but there was no reason for me to freaking cry over the news.

A small rift of wind blew over us, bringing my attention back to the blood I was holding in my hands. I moaned, all tears forgotten, and Gregory made a quick escape back to the fae.

I sped toward the parking lot with the crimson liquid in hand, sloshing it around as I moved faster. I clicked the lock button twice on Gregory's keys so the beep would sound and lead me in the right direction. Gregory's truck was in the first row, and he'd backed into the space, so I'd be able to see him returning. I got into the passenger's seat and threw his keys on the center console.

My hand moved to open the lid on the cup, but I paused as my thoughts caught up to the reality of my situation.

I had almost killed Gregory. I'd wanted to rip his throat out. If the fae hadn't shown up, I would have.

Dread filled me as my hate for vampires now applied to myself.

I was the monster.

CHAPTER 6

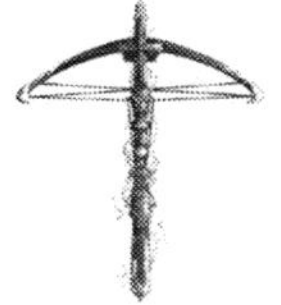

THE SCENT OF BLOOD WAFTED THROUGH MY SENSES. MY fangs elongated once again and cut into my lip, but the wound healed almost immediately.

My hands began to shake as I lifted the lid off. I expected to be disgusted, but as the smell of sweetness overwhelmed me, I nearly panted with excitement.

Still, I hesitated, finding the will to deny myself what I needed most in this new form. How could I be okay with drinking this blood? How could I be a vampire?

It's either this, death, or drinking from the tap, I reminded myself before I could spiral too far out of control.

If I was going to do this, I wanted to take my time,

to have control of my hunger. Yet, as soon as I brought the blood to my lips and the first drops touched my skin, all rational sense went out the window.

My fangs cut into the white material as I finally got what I needed most—crimson liquid that tasted like the most sinful honey I'd ever had.

A shiver raced through me as I squeezed the cup tighter, gulping faster until the container was nearly vertical and I was confident that every drop made its way into my mouth. Even when I was done, my tongue swirled around the rim, wanting more.

I leaned back in the seat and sighed, hating myself for enjoying that moment so thoroughly. I wished I'd hated the taste, but I couldn't lie to myself, not when the craving was still so strong.

Gregory appeared in the parking lot, walking swiftly and with another cup in hand. That man was my savior.

He cautiously opened the door, peeking in before getting too close. "How are you feeling?"

"Better, thanks to you," I said, remaining in my seat even though I wanted to leap across the truck and snatch the other cup I knew he had behind his back.

"I have another one for you if you want it," he said.

"Please," I practically begged.

"I'm going to set it on the console and give you some more privacy."

I forced myself to stay plastered to my chair as he quickly set the cup down, then backed away, slamming the door closed as soon as he was out of the way.

Carefully, I grabbed the blood and lifted the lid. My thirst was still apparent, but I felt more in control of my movements as I brought the container to my lips and took a deep inhale. Instead of the rusty scent I was used to, only sweet nectar filled my senses.

I wanted to be disgusted with myself, but that wasn't happening. Instead, I took healthy gulps of the blood, sighing as a calmness settled over me.

I couldn't believe this had happened to me. I wanted to be glad that Dmitri was dead, but the cost of his death had been the end of my human existence, of any chance at normalcy once I got my vengeance, even if only for a short time.

My head shook as I sensed my emotions starting to spiral again. Becoming a vampire had thrown everything inside me out of whack, and I had to be careful where I let my thoughts travel to until I had more control over myself.

After I finished the cup and set it inside the other, Gregory opened the driver's door. "Better?"

"Much. Thank you. And I'm sorry. About earlier," I said, hoping he wasn't going to make me elaborate.

"Let's just be thankful Lucinda showed up when she did. That was the first time I'd seen her in a long time. Apparently, they're visiting now that things have calmed down on Fae Islands."

"I've never met a fae. Would she really have killed me?" I asked, because I thought fae were supposed to be the nicer species of the supernaturals.

"Absolutely. She's not your normal fae, though. I've heard Finn is like most of them, but I'd never seen him before tonight. Most don't leave the islands too often," Gregory said as he started the truck and headed out of the parking lot.

I stayed quiet as he drove, trying not to focus on the pounding of his heart or the warmth of his blood. Thoughts of Maciah surfaced and what might have happened after I was taken.

"Did Maciah sound okay when you talked to him?" I asked.

"Sounded like it to me, but we weren't on the phone for long," Gregory replied.

When Dmitri had taken me, there had been several vampires with him. Once I was knocked out, they could have attacked the others. My friends could be dead. Maciah could have been hurt.

No, I wouldn't spiral. Everything was going to be fine. They'd all be in LA soon enough and I could see so myself.

"What day is it?" I asked.

"Tuesday," he replied, and I sighed in relief. I'd only been gone since that morning. My hope was that Maciah hadn't done anything he shouldn't have while I'd been missing.

As the truck sped down the interstate, I closed my eyes and did my best to shut off all my senses. Being a new vampire was like PMS on crack.

I wanted to scream and cry and roar, but I had no idea why.

Maciah needed to hurry. I needed him like I'd never needed anyone before. He would know how to make the craziness inside me feel better.

He had to, because there was no way I could live like this for long.

GREGORY STAYED OUTSIDE WHEN WE GOT TO MACIAH'S LA house. I didn't blame him. I wouldn't have wanted to be around me, either. A newborn who could lose control at a moment's notice.

Once I was inside, I went to the fridge searching for more blood. My stomach twisted at the thought that I was already hungry again, but I also hoped that another drink would help to calm my emotions.

Except after four bags of blood, I was still a hot mess, going through emotions like they were a roller coaster ride while I paced the house. I'd inspected every room, closet, and hallway of the big house three times before I ended up on the second-floor balcony facing the back of the property.

I watched the stars until thoughts filtered through of how they lived billions of years, alone up in the sky and in constant conflict with themselves. It was a fact I'd learned from my eighth-grade science teacher and seemed more relatable than ever after becoming a vampire.

My chest rose and fell as I stargazed, and I chuckled at myself. I no longer had to breathe to live. I was undead as a vampire. But muscle memory was a strong thing. I had a feeling there would be lots of things I did and felt that I no longer needed to.

An engine accelerated down the street from the front of the house. Tires skidded as the vehicle forcefully slowed, and my heart soared.

Maciah.

I was out of my seat and downstairs before I could blink. I flung the front door open with unnecessary force, and I heard Gregory jump in surprise from his spot on the porch.

The unfamiliar car jerked to a stop as the driver's door opened. Maciah's dark eyes found mine immediately, and I was in his arms the next moment.

His hands held me tightly to him, the force behind them making me feel safe and cared for. "I'm so sorry, Amersyn," he murmured into my hair.

My arms stayed wrapped around his neck, and I inhaled. The citrus scent I'd known before had nothing on the divineness coming from Maciah now. Hints of vanilla and peppermint intertwined with the fruity scent from before. The combination of the three called to something so explosive within me that I was practically crawling onto him. My lips pressed to his neck, and I moaned. "So good."

He held me firmer, but there was nothing painful about his touch. Only desire filled me as my hands grabbed his long strands and kissed anywhere that I could reach while I was wrapped around him.

I didn't even look for my friends. I could only see and sense Maciah and my need for him.

My control was once again lost, but with Maciah holding me, I wasn't as frightened at the loss. I trusted him to keep me safe.

As I clung to him, he carried us into the house and directly into the room we'd shared before. My core tightened in excitement. I wanted all of Maciah. Right then and for as long as time allowed.

Except when he pulled back from me, desire was the last thing I could see in his eyes.

They were dark and tortured and raging, even as he held me and gently stroked my cheek.

"Amersyn, I'm going to help you, but I need your assistance in order to do so," he said softly.

I began pulling at his dress shirt. "Gladly."

His jaw tensed. "Not like that."

Anger ignited within me. I released my hold on him, landed on my feet, and shoved him back a good ten feet into the wall before crossing my arms and sneering at him. "Do you not want me now that I'm a monster? Was my human body the only thing you cared about *protecting* before?"

He raised his hands and took careful steps toward me. "My feelings for you haven't changed, Amersyn, but you're not yourself right now and I won't take advantage of you."

I laughed in his face. "Always Mr. Chivalrous. Why don't you try being Mr. Sexy for once?"

"Your emotions are on a high from the transition, but we can work through them without doing anything you might regret. You've probably been experiencing ups and downs all night, right?"

I glared at him. I didn't want him to be right. I just wanted him to want me.

"I'll take your silence as a yes. This happens to about half of the newborns, and it's why it takes longer to get some settled. I'm going to help you, but I need you to trust me. Do you trust me, Amersyn?" Maciah's eyes lightened as he reached for me.

His skin always seemed colder than mine before. Not icy, but not warm either. Now, as he took my hand in his, its warmth filled me with renewed passion. Maciah was safe.

"I trust you."

He grabbed my other hand. "Close your eyes, take a deep breath, and tell me what you feel."

I did as he said, licking my lips as the hint of vanilla coming from him coated my tongue. Searching inside myself, I was vulnerable with Maciah for the first time, and thankful we were alone.

"I feel out of control. I'm hungry, but not for food or blood. I'm afraid of who I am and what I will do. I'm ashamed of the hatred I lived by for so many years. I'm angry that Dmitri was able to kill me. That I couldn't protect myself."

His palms rubbed over my arms, then he stepped closer. "Find your control and you can overcome your hunger. You are strong and capable, Amersyn. Nobody has ever controlled you. Don't let the venom flowing inside you do so now. Overcome the need, and there isn't anything else you can't do."

He was so close to me. His breath mixed with my own as my lungs worked faster, but not for survival.

I raised my hands, covering Maciah's chest as I opened my eyes again. He was staring down at me, and desire for only him thrummed through me once more. I wanted to devour him, and I would, but I knew what he meant about gaining control.

There was a difference between taking what I

wanted and getting what I wanted because I'd earned it.

His head lowered to mine. "That's my girl," he whispered.

I closed the distance between us, pressing my lips to his and gripping his rumpled shirt. He opened his mouth to me, and I pushed closer, turning him until he was standing in front of the bed. With one soft shove, Maciah fell onto the mattress.

"Do you sense your strength?" he asked while looking up at me.

"I do."

"How does that make you feel?"

"Like I don't want to talk. Only act," I answered truthfully as I climbed on top of him, straddling his hips.

My fingers moved to unbutton his shirt, then took pleasure in tearing the cotton in two with the smallest effort.

Maciah was grinning at me. I thought he'd fight my need based on his earlier words, but he'd yet to put a stop to my intentions.

I leaned back, undoing his belt and pants before meeting his eyes. "Are you going to stop me?" I asked.

"Are you in control?" he countered.

I closed my eyes, doing what he asked of me before. My insatiable desire for Maciah was calmer. I wasn't in a hurry. I still needed him, but I wasn't out of control. I wasn't emotional. I knew exactly what I wanted and needed.

"I am."

He smirked. "Then I have no reason to stop you."

I took his permission seriously and had his pants off in the next moment. I was fully dressed while Maciah lay gloriously naked on the bed before me.

He leaned up onto his elbows, muscles rippling along his stomach from the movements. "What do you want now?"

My eyes followed the trail of sparse hair down between his hips and to the dick that twitched under my appraisal. I licked my lips and moved to my knees. I wanted to make Maciah as needy as I was.

I swirled my tongue over his swollen tip and sucked the head into my mouth as his hands rested on my head, guiding me as I took him deeper into my mouth. Every inch of Maciah would be mine.

With each thrust of his hips, I sucked harder, wanting to make him feel even a sliver of what was building within my core. Heightened emotions or not, I'd been fighting my need for this vampire for too long now.

As I felt him tense beneath my lips, Maciah lifted me off of him, and I was suddenly on the bed, being undressed.

My clothes were already tattered, so there seemed

to be no hesitation from Maciah about ripping them apart at the seams.

"Are you still in control?" he asked while hovering above me.

I nodded, so sure of myself in that moment. I might not be once we left this room, but with just me and Maciah, I had no thoughts or feelings trying to choke the air from me.

He flipped us, so I was once again on top. He was letting me take the lead with how far things went, which I appreciated. I felt comfortable that I could stop now and there would be no pressure from him for anything more until I was ready.

But I was damned glad I had no intentions of stopping.

Maciah's hands were on my hips, and I stared down at him, tracing my fingers over his chest as I tried to decide what I wanted next.

I was in control. Becoming a vampire wouldn't change who I was at heart. I could prevent that from happening. I hadn't had sex with Maciah, because I hadn't been mentally prepared to cross that line before, but there was no going back to who I was before. Not now. Even if I'd already known that, a part of me had still resisted. That was the part that had kept me from fully allowing Maciah in.

Staring at him now, I could see Maciah had

suffered right alongside me when I'd been taken, even though we'd been a thousand miles apart.

I bent over, pressing my lips to his as I lifted my hips up. Maciah's hands guided me over his dick, and the hardened length pressed at my core while I pushed down.

As he entered me, I gasped, and Maciah nipped at my lips, stealing my attention back. "Focus on me," he whispered.

Our gazes connected, and I once again did as he asked, trusting him completely. Neither of us blinked as he slowly pressed into me. I nearly died from need, but not once did I second guess my actions.

By the time I had taken all of him in, I could feel my first orgasm already building. I leaned forward, putting pressure where I wanted it most, and rode the waves, taking full control.

Maciah's hips countered my movements, hitting the mark with every move until I tightened around him, arching my body and tilting my head back. My muscles clenched almost painfully, and my body tingled with ecstasy until I was forced to let go of the control I'd fought to get back.

The intensity that raced through my core extended out, starting slowly before exploding all the way to my fingers and toes, causing me to cry out in euphoria.

"I've got you, Amersyn." Maciah's voice was a beacon as I came down from the high.

He'd managed to reverse our roles without me realizing it during my daze. I opened my eyes to find him staring down at me. His knuckles caressed my cheek. "Still in control?"

"Absolutely." I gave him a lopsided grin. Even though there had been a moment when I'd let go, the fact that I'd been able to rein my emotions in so quickly afterward proved that what Maciah had been saying before was working.

He moved above me, leaning down to kiss me senseless. My nails dug into his shoulders as he used one hand to lift my hips and plunge deeper with the new angle. I moaned into his mouth, soaking in the bliss until Maciah began moving faster and harder above me.

I clung to him, arching my spine and tilting my head back, letting him momentarily turn me into nothing more than hormones and neediness.

I'd been afraid to let Maciah in before, but now that I'd had him so completely, I knew there was no letting him go.

CHAPTER 7

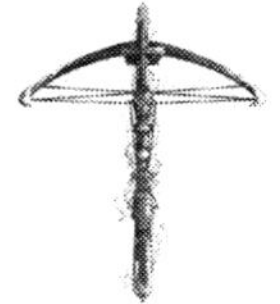

MACIAH TRIED TO PULL HIMSELF UP WHEN WE WERE both sated, but I hooked my ankles around his legs, holding him to me.

"If you get up, then this moment is over," I murmured.

"It doesn't have to be if you don't want it to be. You are in control, Amersyn."

He kept saying that, but I was beginning to realize he wasn't being as literal as I'd first taken him. The sex might be over, but I didn't have to forget the feelings he'd drawn out of me during the intimacy. I could hold on to those for as long as I wanted.

Still, I kept him close to me. If he got up, then we'd have to talk about the other things I'd happily avoided before. Like the fact I was now a vampire and I'd died earlier that evening. I wasn't even sure if he knew I'd killed Dmitri.

I wanted him to know everything that had happened since we separated that morning, but being a vampire was multifaceted. I didn't like every enhancement I'd been experiencing.

He gripped my chin. "Hey, it's going to be okay. All things considered, you're doing amazing."

I snorted. "I almost killed Gregory. My emotions until you arrived were that of nightmares for someone like me. I mauled you the moment I laid eyes on you. Yeah, that's not what I call amazing."

"Give yourself credit, Amersyn. The fact that you are a newborn and made it to the club without killing anyone shows how strong your will is. You might not have felt in control, but deep down, where it mattered most, you were. More importantly, I know if we get out of this bed, you still will be."

I'd been so sure of who I was and what I wanted just a month ago. My purpose had been laid out and there was never a thought about deviating from it.

Now that things weren't so crystal clear, I found myself second-guessing who I was and what I was going to do about it.

Maciah's words shined a much-needed light on the fears that I'd let plague my consciousness. I was still Amersyn Holt. I could continue hunting vampires even if I was one. I would still be able to get the vengeance I sought for my family.

I leaned up and kissed Maciah. "Thank you."

"A smart woman once reminded me that being your protector was about more than keeping you safe. I'm just doing my part."

"Is this also part of the protector description?" My hips raised between us as I teased him.

"Not even close. Being with you is a bonus I never expected. Nothing between us is out of obligation. Not a single feeling," he said, brushing wisps of my ebony hair back.

"I wouldn't be here if I thought otherwise." I released my hold on him, feeling better about moving forward and facing my new reality head on.

I might have had a month to come to grips with becoming a vampire *someday*, but having that day appear so soon was unexpected.

"I'm going to take a shower. I washed up a little while I was waiting for you, but scalding hot water will do me some good," I said, silently hoping he'd join me.

"Rachel packed a bag for you. I'm going to go grab that and let them all know you're okay." He reached for me, a deep crease forming between his eyes. "I wasn't the only one losing my mind when we couldn't find you."

There was a tension radiating from him that I'd

never sensed from anyone before—an underlying fury and fear that he'd either hidden from me before or that I'd been too hyped up to sense. Likely the latter.

"I'm sorry you were scared. I had just wanted to go for a run outside. I purposely stayed on the property with no intention of leaving. I don't know if some of your guards were in on it, but one minute they were posted at each corner and then the next, they weren't. I tried to fight back, but Dmitri had several vampires with him. Though, we won't ever have to worry about that bloodsucker again." I could feel my emotions rising when I thought about Dmitri. Even though he was no longer alive, the thought of that monster had my muscles coiling to attack and my adrenaline increasing as I recalled jabbing the stake into his heart and the enjoyment of watching him turn to ash.

I leaned my head against Maciah's chest, taking a deep breath to prevent myself from spiraling.

"How did you kill him?" Maciah asked, a bit of hesitancy in his tone.

I looked back up "He had me in a room alone, and I had a lot of motivation. The idiot hadn't even searched me before tying me to the chair. I had one small stake tucked into a pocket at the back of my pants. After he started bringing out torture devices and even stabbed me in the shoulder and leg, I wasn't going to let him keep at it for long."

"You shouldn't have had to go through what you did on your own. I should have been there with you, especially when the change began," Maciah said. His guilt was loud and clear, pulsing around us like the wind.

"Even though I lost my cool, I think it was best I had to handle things on my own," I said, knowing I would have panicked more if I hadn't been so focused on getting somewhere safe and back to Maciah.

He pressed his forehead to mine, gripping my elbows. "You have no idea how grateful I was when Zeke got Gregory's call. We had no idea where to go or who took you. I never want to feel that way again."

"And I hope you never have to."

He smirked, still staring at me. "I should probably put some pants on."

"Or you could join me in the shower."

"As tempting as that is, Zeke, Rachel, and Nikki are the only reasons I didn't go on a killing spree. The least I can do in return is let them know you're okay."

I cringed. "Given I can hear them chatting outside, I'm sure they're fully aware of how okay I am right now. Vampire hearing isn't all people make it seem."

Maciah lifted my chin. "After living with over forty other vampires, I assure you, they've gotten good at tuning out the sounds they don't want to hear."

Something told me Rachel and Nikki would have been listening for anything to do with me until they had their confirmation. I wasn't going to be living this one down anytime soon.

He pulled away and grabbed his pants, leaving the ruined shirt on the ground, and I headed to the connected bathroom.

I'd yet to really inspect myself. I hadn't been ready when I was by myself earlier, but after Maciah helped bring some clarity to the craziness flowing through me, it was time to see what I'd become.

I turned the shower on first, then faced the mirror and gasped.

Bright red eyes stared back at me instead of the muddy-red I was used to seeing on the other vampires I didn't want to kill. One deep breath in, another one out. Okay, that wasn't the end of the world. I could wear contacts if needed. No need to freak out. Yet.

The next thing I noticed was my skin. It was smooth and free of flaws. No scars or blemishes to be seen. The color was still the same as before. I'd always been fair-skinned and unable to hold a tan. Maybe there had been a reason for that.

My hair was thicker and shinier than I'd ever seen it, but still black as the night. I was still me, just a little more polished around the edges and redder in the eyes. I could live with that as long as my emotions didn't get out of control again.

The mirror was beginning to steam, so I turned back to the shower. It was time to wash the day off me and see what life as a vampire was truly like.

I SPENT ANOTHER HOUR IN THE ROOM. THE CONFIDENCE I'd been gaining faltered more every time I saw my red eyes, yet I couldn't stop myself from going back to the mirror to see them over and over again.

I didn't want to be a monster. I didn't want others to think I was either.

As my thoughts kept spinning in circles, I went down in a tailspin while wondering how many red-eyed vampires I had killed that might not have been what they seemed.

It was one thing to think only the good ones had darker red eyes, but knowing that wasn't the case for me, it had to be the same for others.

Maciah was in and out of the room, reassuring me that everything would be fine if I just came out, but he wouldn't pressure me to do something I wasn't ready for. He had even offered to send the others on without us, but I shut that idea down immediately.

I wanted to see them all—badly—but I'd gotten in my own head again. Damn, how long was this madness going to last?

One breath in, another out. I just had to keep repeating that to myself. Every time I did, things got a little easier, but I still hadn't made it beyond the bedroom door.

A knock sounded, followed by Rachel's voice. "It's me and Nikki. We're just checking on you."

Normally, my steadfast friend waltzed right into my room. This time, she waited for me to speak. Gave me time to send them away if that was what I thought was best for me.

I knew it wasn't, so I found my determination, heading to the door and opening it up.

They stood there, once again waiting for me to make the first move. This time, my emotions didn't get the better of me. Now that I could see their faces, the fear I'd been holding on to began to dissipate. I didn't even know where it had originated from, but I was slowly finding my way back.

"Hi," I said, making it extra awkward with an added wave.

"We missed you so much." Rachel gathered me

into her arms, and I hugged her back. "Oh, you're strong!"

Nikki stole me from her. "That's what happens when you officially become a vampire." She winked at me. "We don't have to stay, but I couldn't keep her chained any longer."

Rachel shoved her. "I heard that."

"You were supposed to. That's payback for all of the pacing you did outside," Nikki droned.

"Excuse me for caring about my friend while she is going through something huge." Rachel crossed her arms and glared.

I wrapped an arm around them both. "I missed you both. I'm sorry I couldn't come downstairs. It was just…"

"A lot? Overwhelming? Stressful? Terrifying?" Rachel said, attempting to finish my sentence.

"Something like that," I said with a small smile, "but now that you're both in the room with me, it's not so bad. I think it's my eyes. They're bothering me a lot more than I expected."

Nikki shushed me. "The color will calm down in a week or two once your human blood has been filtered out by the donated stuff. How long has it been since the last time you ate?"

"Uhhh, no idea. When Gregory picked me up," I answered. I didn't even know what time it was then.

Both of their eyes widened at me. "You've gone

over eight hours without feeding right after turning?" Rachel gasped.

I shook my head. "No, wait. I had four bags while I was waiting for you guys. I finished the last one about half an hour before you pulled into the driveway, so it's only been a few hours."

"That's better, but still, it's no wonder you're pent-up and nervous. You need more blood. It will help give you some chill. Most newborns are like human babies. They eat every two hours. I'll grab you another cup," Nikki said and was out the door before I could give an opinion.

"Maciah must have been too distracted to remember that," Rachel added, waggling her eyebrows at me.

"Yeah, maybe. What time is it anyway?" I asked, hoping to steer the subject away from the sex everyone knew I'd just had. That fact might have also played a factor in me not wanting to leave the room.

Rachel checked her phone. "It's 4:16 in the morning."

Damn, and I wasn't even tired. At least this particular vampire perk didn't suck. There was a lot I could get done if I never slept again.

Nikki reappeared with two travel mugs in her hand. "One for now and one for later."

"Thank you." I took the nearest cup, and she set the other one down. As soon as I tilted the mug back, my fangs grew, and my thirst flared at the sweet scent. I took three large gulps, getting half of the contents down in one go before deciding to slow my pace, considering I had an audience. I knew they wouldn't judge, but I was still uncomfortable feeling like a savage.

"Seriously, though. How are you doing with everything? Maciah said you killed Dmitri, so that's at least something good out of all of this," Rachel said.

I nodded. "Yeah, but he killed me at the same time, so it's definitely bittersweet. Some minutes, I feel like I'm handling it pretty well, and others, not so much. How are things back at the mansion?" I didn't really want to rehash my emotions. Maybe another day, but for now, I just wanted to keep putting one foot in front of the other. Plus, I'd asked Maciah about this earlier and he never got the chance to answer me.

"There was a pile of ash scattered across the wet grass where one of the guards should have been and the other is missing. We can't be certain, but the second one was probably working with Dmitri. He was newer to our nest. We should have been more careful with who we chose for watch duty, but we didn't have a lot of options either. Between sending people to look for Viktor and Silas and watching our own nest, help was getting slim," Rachel said.

I hated to hear one of them died, but I also wasn't surprised. Not about that or the fact that one of them might have let Dmitri and his men in.

"Speaking of home, we should probably head back soon. We're supposed to be getting another big storm before Spring starts to make an appearance. If we don't make it before the snow starts to fall in Portland, we might not be able to fly home," Nikki said.

"You're just in a hurry to get back so you can leave," Rachel said.

"Where are you going?" I asked Nikki after I finished my first mug of blood, then I turned to grab the bag Maciah had brought in for me.

"Well, I was supposed to come back here. I like the weather down here a hell of a lot better, but I'm going to stick around a little longer up North," Nikki answered.

I couldn't fault her for that reasoning. Portland was downright depressing in the wintertime. Sunshine was life. Not that I'd get to fully enjoy that feeling any longer.

I shook my head. I wasn't going there. I needed to focus on not feeling sorry for myself if I was going to keep control over these vampire emotions. I couldn't spiral again. At least, not so soon.

Rachel and Nikki had given me a moment of normalcy. Maciah had given me…so much more than that. That was what mattered most. I was different, but I was okay.

With the bag Maciah had brought tightly grasped in my hand, I took a deep breath, grateful I no longer smelled the scent of death when I was near my new friends. Instead, Rachel's scent was sweet like lavender while Nikki's was spicier like cinnamon. Fitting for both of them.

Maciah was at my side before we entered the living room. He took the bag from me and grabbed my hand that wasn't holding the other mug of blood. "I'm sorry I didn't think of feeding you earlier. Are you okay?"

I smiled. "I am."

Zeke approached, seeming hesitant to get too close.

"Come here, Zeke," I said, letting go of Maciah and pulling the other vampire into a hug. He wanted for nothing more than a family. A hug was the least I could do.

Zeke's body shook as we embraced. "I'm a sucker for hugs."

"I suspected as much," I murmured before we pulled apart.

"I'm glad you're still in one piece and we have you back. It wasn't fun without you," Zeke added.

"I'll try not to get kidnapped again," I replied.

Maciah led me ahead. "Alright, let's get going."

"You got it, Pilot," Zeke said, blurring ahead of us. Though, with my new eyes, I could clearly see every step he took.

I glanced up at Maciah. "Did he just call you Pilot?"

He shrugged. "Who buys a plane and doesn't learn how to fly it?"

"Apparently, not you," I deadpanned.

Freaking rich vampires.

CHAPTER 8

Maciah flew us back to Oregon. I was a nervous wreck at first, my heightened emotions nearly getting the best of me again, but after a few sips from the second travel mug of blood, I was back in control.

When we landed, the sun had already risen, but the sky was heavily clouded due to the incoming storm, so I was saved from discovering how sensitive I was going to be to the UV rays for the foreseeable future. I was happy to leave some things for later after the hell I'd been through during the last twenty-four hours.

The mansion came into view, and my eyes watched every shadow as we pulled into the driveway. After being taken from the property, I knew I had to be on guard at all times moving forward. We still had Silas and Viktor to consider.

"How about we go up to your room?" Rachel suggested to me as we got out of the SUV.

"Don't we need to figure out our next move?" I asked.

She looped an arm through mine, forcing a smile to her face. "We can do that upstairs."

Something was off, and I wanted to know what it was. "I'd rather go to Maciah's office."

Maciah was at my side before I finished my sentence. The back of his hand brushed my cheek. "I left a mess here yesterday. I need to go check on some things and then we'll all meet, okay?"

His voice was soft and patient, but I also sensed an underlying nervousness in his words. Something was going on that I wasn't being included in.

"I can help if you'd like," I said.

"I've got it handled. I'll see you as soon as I'm done," Maciah replied, kissing my forehead and moving past me, toward the house.

My eyes cast to Rachel and Nikki, who were looking everywhere but at me. My rage was rising. I wanted to punch something. Or someone. That wasn't who I was before, though, and not who I wanted to be as a vampire. I refused to be a loose screw everyone had to be worried around.

I left Rachel and Nikki in the garage and ran to my room. Running at full speed was getting easier every time I did it, and I practically flew up the stairs before slowing down to avoid crashing into my door.

As I glanced around the room, I saw that all my drawers were open, as were the doors to the closet and bathroom. Someone had gone through everything I owned.

One breath in. Another out. I would not rage because of this. Everything was fine.

Nikki's hand clasped my shoulder. "Are you good?"

I nodded, afraid to speak because I wanted to scream.

Rachel closed the door and came around to face me. "You're doing incredible, Amersyn."

"As opposed to what?" I sneered.

"Do you remember when you first arrived and Maciah was busy with some of our newest recruits?" she asked, and I nodded. "That's how it is with a lot of the vampires we bring in. They have to be contained for days, sometimes weeks, depending on the state we find them in. The fact that we haven't had to lock you up is huge."

I chuckled. "I'd like to see you try."

"And someone needs more blood." Nikki disappeared as I glared at Rachel.

"You're not angry with me, Amersyn. You care about me, and you won't hurt me," she said, stepping closer.

"Do I? All I can remember right now is all the times you drove me mad," I snapped.

She gripped my shoulders. "I am your friend. I love you. I won't leave your side until you have this under control."

Nikki returned with three glasses and a couple of blood bags in her arms. "Let's see if we can unearth the Amersyn that doesn't want to murder us."

As she tore the bag open, I nearly fell to my knees. The call of the blood was powerful. More so than any other time before then.

"You're burning through your human blood quicker than we suspected. We're going to help you as much as we can," Rachel said, standing next to me.

"You guys assumed I was going to lose control before we even got back, didn't you?" I asked, eagerly accepting the glass from Nikki.

"We did. You were fidgeting, and your eyes weren't focusing on any one thing for very long. Even though we made you upset, you coming to your room was exactly what we hoped for. You don't need to deal with anything extra right now. Just focus on you and remember that you're somewhere safe," Nikki answered.

Did I feel safe in the mansion? I was familiar with the walls around me, but I wasn't sure safety was something I associated with them any longer.

"How long is this supposed to last?" I asked after a few sips.

Rachel shrugged. "It's different for every newborn, but we aren't lying when we say you're doing great. I'm sure being an heir helps with that."

I ignored the compliment. "Why did you guys go through all of my stuff?"

"Maciah was running out of options to figure out where you went. He didn't know what he was looking for. He just needed something to do," Nikki answered, and my heart hurt even more for my protector.

Maciah was good at hiding his true emotions from me, and that was something we were going to need to chat about. He didn't need to be afraid to show me how he felt, even when it was bad.

"Am I supposed to be different from you guys because an original created me? I know my blood could boost Silas's strength and heal him from the dark magic he messed with, but is there more I still don't know?" I asked, needing to be aware of any other surprises that might be coming.

"It's possible. Darius had the ability of compulsion, and I know more of the originals could do other things like read minds, control emotions, and project thoughts, among other lesser-known abilities," Nikki answered.

"So, anything to do with the mind sounds like

could be possible. Does the ability work on vampires and humans alike?" I asked.

"Humans, definitely. Vampires, with practice and age, usually. It depends on how old and experienced they are in comparison to the person trying to manipulate them. Vampires can live forever if they're careful. Silas is somewhere between six and seven hundred years old. He wouldn't be an easy one to influence, but a new vampire would be," Rachel said.

"How will I know if I have one of these abilities?" The panic inside me was already calming, but I couldn't decide if that was because of the blood or learning more about who I was going to be. Possibly both.

"That might be a question for Maciah to answer. Neither of us knew the originals. Maciah is the only one around here who had met your father," Rachel replied.

I went to my bed, sitting up against the headboard and wishing I could sleep and turn my mind off for a while. Energy was bouncing around inside me, but I was so tired at the same time. Mental exhaustion was a beast.

Rachel and Nikki joined me. "It's going to be okay, Am. You'll hang out in here for a few days and things will settle. After that, we'll find Silas or Viktor, whoever is closest," Rachel said.

"My bet is on Silas. He never has been known for his patience," Nikki added.

I didn't know either murderous vampire, but I had to agree with Nikki.

"Do I really have to stay in this room until I don't need blood to keep me calm?" I asked, already feeling cabin fever setting in.

Rachel grimaced. "Try not to think of it that way. The storm is coming. Most of us will be staying in anyway. I'll bring games and movies and we'll make the most of it."

Nikki patted her on the shoulder. "She's not going to want to spend her evenings with us, Rach."

"Why not?" Rachel asked, offended. "Oh, never mind."

Nikki laughed and I just shook my head, looking anywhere but at either of them.

Nikki's foot kicked my knee. "We won't pry, like we said before, but don't be embarrassed of what you've found with Maciah. We're all searching for the same thing. Living forever isn't as fun as it sounds when you're doing it alone."

"Vampires don't have mates like shifters, right? Maciah being bound to protect me is something different than that?" I asked, wanting to make sure I really did understand.

Rachel shook her head. "You and Maciah are definitely one-of-a-kind. And correct, the rest of us don't have mates, but with our enhanced senses, it's easy to know when someone has good intentions or is just looking for something temporary."

At least all of the overwhelming crap I was feeling wouldn't always be something that drove me mad. I'd done a decent job tuning out the noises from my new hearing, but the rest of the senses were harder to control.

I took another long drink of blood, then leaned back against the headboard again as I closed my eyes. "Tell me something that has nothing to do with vampires," I said.

"The unicorn is the national animal of Scotland," Rachel said much too quickly to be random.

I peeked at her through half-closed eyes, expecting to find a smile on her face or something to indicate humor, but she was as straight-faced as ever.

I chuckled. "Right."

"Seriously. I read it in Cosmopolitan," she added.

I laughed even harder. "You read Cosmo in your spare time?"

"Not always, but sometimes when I'm bored. Don't judge me. That's not what friends do," she said with a huff.

I leaned forward, resting my hand on her knee. "You're right. I'm sorry. That is a very random and interesting fact and definitely has nothing to do with vampires."

Rain began pelting the windows behind us. "The storm has arrived," Nikki said with disappointment.

Yeah, I wasn't at all excited about that, either. Just because they'd tried to use the crappy weather as partial justification for staying in my room didn't mean I'd forgotten I was basically being forced to hide away.

I understood why, but that didn't mean I was happy about it.

CHAPTER 9

FIVE DAYS PASSED BEFORE I WAS ALLOWED TO BE AROUND other vampires besides Maciah, Rachel, Nikki, and Zeke, and another three days before they deemed I was ready to leave the mansion and resume normal activities like working out. During that time, I'd almost broken Rachel's arm, tried to choke out Nikki, and punched Maciah more times than I cared to recall. Zeke was the only one to successfully avoid one of my outbursts. Considering I'd stabbed him once before, I figured he already knew better.

I'd also laughed and cried and been more insatiable than I expected. Thankfully, no matter how many bruises I left on Maciah, he was happy to oblige with the latter issue. Orgasms from my protector were better than any amount of blood they kept feeding me.

Sleep finally came for me that evening after I'd been told that the following day would be the first time I'd be able to get out. Relief had settled my mind enough that I was able to get the rest I'd been missing. Even though I no longer needed sleep, turning my thoughts off for a few hours meant everything to me.

When I woke, I found Maciah leaning over me and grinning. "What has you so happy?" I asked.

"I found someone who knows something about Silas," he said, and I nearly headbutted him when I shot out of bed.

"What did they tell you?" We'd only found dead ends wherever we looked for information.

"He wouldn't say over the phone. He wants to meet me at Nyx tonight," Maciah answered.

"Like right now tonight, or later like tomorrow?" I had no idea what time it was, but I was pretty sure it was after midnight.

"Right now. I was going to leave you a note, but you began to stir when I opened the door. I'll be back as soon as I meet this guy," he said.

"I'm coming with you." I was already scrambling out of bed. I could be dressed in mere seconds with my new speed.

Maciah grabbed my arm. "I don't think that's a good idea, Amersyn."

My eyes narrowed on him. "I've been caged for

over a week. I have passed every test you've thrown at me the last two days. I'm going with you." My voice was even, there were no spikes in my emotions, and I hadn't had blood in hours. I was more than capable of leaving the house without having anything go wrong because of me.

"Please, stay here," he said, eyes pleading with me.

"I can't do that. You should have left without saying goodbye if you wanted that and you know it," I replied.

As he stood there, I wasted no time getting dressed. Using my vampire speed, I had on black jeans, my favorite boots, and a dark green top. Technically, I didn't need stakes any longer—I could kill vampires with my bare hands—but I still tucked a couple into each boot before thinking about my contacts Nikki had given me.

We were going to a supernatural club, so they weren't necessary, but given how red my eyes were, it would make me feel better to dim the color with brown contacts. When I appeared in front of the mirror, though, they were no longer bright red like before. The color finally had deeper browns bleeding through, calming the brightness of the previous crimson tint to my eyes. Still, I wanted to be certain they didn't brighten back to monster red on my first venture out.

I had the contacts in and was out of the bathroom within ten seconds given that I didn't have to do anything with my hair. I was extra thankful that my new vampire hair rarely got tangled and no longer required minutes of brushing to tame.

"Let's go," I said with a grin as I returned to Maciah less than a minute after I'd gone to my closet.

"I don't have a choice here, do I?" he asked with a sigh of defeat.

I pressed up onto my toes and kissed him on the cheek. "No, but it's adorable that you thought you might."

Nikki burst through my door. "Did you hear—"

I cut her off. "That we're going to Nyx. I sure did."

Nikki glanced between the two of us, seeming unsure of how to respond. She had a lot of respect for her nest leader and didn't act as casual with him as she did with me and Rachel.

"Rachel is going, too. I need the two of you to stay with Amersyn while I speak with the informant. Be at the car in five minutes," Maciah grumbled and headed toward the door.

"Hey," I called, and he turned back. "Thank you." They were only two words, but they were sincere, and I hoped my tone and the softness in my eyes portrayed that.

He sighed, coming back to me with three quick strides. He grabbed my face and kissed me for several seconds before pulling back. "You're welcome."

Maciah disappeared, and I turned to Nikki, who was fanning her face. "Hot, dude."

"And all mine," I replied with a smirk.

"About damn time you said that with confidence. Now, let's go get Rachel," she said.

We left my room and headed to Rachel's, but she wasn't there. "Kitchen?" I suggested.

"Good call." Nikki ran that way, and I was right on her heels. Wind created from my speed was pushing my hair back and I smiled as it once again seemed like I was flying with my feet moving so fast underneath me.

The moment was over quickly as we slowed in the hallway before the kitchen. Rachel's giggling sounded, then someone muttered something. We came around the corner only to find Rachel by herself.

"Umm, whatcha up to?" Nikki asked.

Rachel ran a hand through her hair. "Oh, nothing. Just grabbing a drink before we go. You heard we're leaving for Nyx, right?"

"We sure did. How did you hear? Maybe from whoever was just in here with you?" Nikki pressed.

"I saw Zeke on my way down here and I was

alone before you arrived," she said without meeting Nikki's direct gaze.

I took a deep inhale to see if I could scent anyone familiar, but there were too many spices in the kitchen along with the normal vampire scents to figure out why she was lying.

"You're full of shit, but we don't have time to grill you. Let's go before they leave without us," Nikki said.

Rachel visibly relaxed as Nikki disappeared. I joined her as we headed for the garage. "I'm all for having privacy—you know that—but don't completely shut us out if you've got something big happening," I said.

She waved a hand. "It's nothing. If there was anything to tell, I would."

"Okay. I trust you. And Nikki will understand, too. We were just surprised."

"It won't happen again," she said as we got to the garage.

Yeah, that might have been what she hoped, but nothing ever worked out that way. At least in my experience.

Maciah was in the driver's seat of his white Mercedes with Zeke in the passenger seat. Nikki was just sliding into the back as we stepped down the stairs into the garage. We joined her, and the tension in the car was thick.

"Do we have a problem?" Maciah asked.

"Nope," Rachel answered first with a forced smile.

Zeke turned around in his seat, glancing first at Rachel, then at me and Nikki. "Drive. We only have twenty minutes to get there before he leaves," he said to Maciah, even though his gaze was leveled on us for several more beats.

Well, this was starting out fun. I was finally feeling more like myself and everyone else was going off the rails.

Zeke thankfully turned the radio on, so I hummed along to the tune and watched out the window, enjoying that the lights no longer passed by in blurry streaks while Maciah drove eighty on the interstate.

We pulled up to the club ten minutes later. It was almost one in the morning, but there were plenty of cars coming and going around us. The valet took the keys from Maciah, and I spotted the same bouncer at the entrance as the last time we were there.

"Welcome back, Mr. West. Would you like us to get a private booth set up for you?" CeCe asked.

"I won't be here long enough for that," he said, strolling past her without waiting for any other response.

He was in full vampire leader mode, and it was sexy as hell.

CeCe saw me and raised a brow. "Did you get that membership?"

"We'll take care of it as soon as Maciah's business is finished," Zeke said, pulling me along so we didn't lose Maciah in the club.

Maciah was stopped just ahead of us, talking with two people I didn't recognize. A woman with long brown hair and hazel eyes, and a man who was well over six feet tall with light brown hair and blue eyes. They were both dressed casually and seemed completely out of their element.

Maciah was shaking hands with the man I could scent was a wolf shifter.

"What are you doing in Portland?" Maciah asked.

"Cait needed to get the last of her things from her storage units, and Embry convinced her to check this place out while we were in Oregon," the man answered with a grimace.

The woman with him smiled and waved at me. "I'm Cait. This is Roman. We live down in East Texas. I didn't see you before."

I wasn't sure what "before" she was talking about, but she was friendly enough. "I'm Amersyn. I just joined with this nest." She didn't need to know I was a new vampire.

Cait smiled at Zeke. "You still haven't come by. I meant what I said about an open invitation to our pack. I'm sure Sam would like to see you."

Rachel tensed next to me. I cocked my head at her while she was doing her best to play it cool. "Don't you guys need to get inside?" she asked.

"It was good to see you both, but Rachel is right, and it seems you were just leaving anyway," Zeke said, moving ahead.

Maciah turned to me. "Stay at the bar and don't talk to anyone until we're back."

"Is something going down? Do you guys want help?" Cait asked, seeming almost hopeful that there would be some action.

"No, we're good here," Rachel said, but Maciah countered her.

"If you're not in a hurry, I wouldn't mind talking to Roman when I'm done," he said.

"You were there when we needed you. We're happy to stick around," the alpha wolf said.

Great. I sensed some heavy awkwardness while we waited.

Maciah and Zeke entered the main part of the bar, and Roman glanced between all the women he'd suddenly been stuck with. "I'm just going to go keep an eye on things out there. You four head to the bar." Roman was gone before anyone could object.

Nikki gestured forward. "Shall we?"

"Please. I have the longest drive ahead of me and some fun before we leave tomorrow is just what I need to survive. I should have known better than to come to a club with only me and my mate," Cait said with a sigh.

"Why didn't you guys fly back home?" I asked. Maybe wolves had a thing with planes I didn't know about.

"We did on the way here, but I had stuff in storage that was too big to get on a plane with. We thought it would be fun to drive back, but I'm seriously reconsidering that now," Cait answered.

Rachel still seemed off kilter, so I tried to keep the conversation going by myself while Nikki played lookout. "When did you move to Texas?" I asked.

"End of last summer. I was traveling a lot before meeting Roman. Things are finally calm in our pack for the most part, so I'm only now getting the rest of my stuff."

"Something happen?" I asked.

She waved a hand. "That's a long story I'd rather not rehash. Rachel was there for part of it, though. Maybe she can fill you in later?"

I nudged my friend. "Yeah, maybe she can. Sorry, give us a second."

I was not supposed to be playing hostess to a wolf shifter I'd never met before. Rachel needed to snap out of it.

Grabbing on to her arm, I pulled her a few feet away and Nikki followed us. "What's going on with you?" I whisper-hissed.

"Nothing." Rachel crossed her arms, and I gave her a pointed stare. "Seriously. It's nothing."

"You're the nicest person I've ever met, and you're being seriously rude to Cait. Is there something about her I should know?" I didn't want to make friends with someone who wasn't as good as they acted.

Nikki cut in. "I think I know."

"Know what?" I asked.

"Zeke was in the kitchen with Rachel."

My eyes widened. "While that's interesting, we're not talking about that right now."

"But it's relatable. You see, this wolf pack intrigued Zeke. He left our nest a few times to help them out. Given what I've put together since we left the house, Rachel has a thing with Zeke, and Cait just invited him once again to her pack. How do you think that made our girl feel?"

Rachel's face turned a shade of red that I didn't think was possible given her vampire makeup. "Is she right?" I asked.

She shrugged, refusing to deny or confirm the information.

"Okay, that makes more sense, but I doubt Cait is being malicious about inviting Zeke back. She seems nice," I said.

Cait's head appeared right next to mine. "I am nice, and I have wolf hearing, too." She looked at

Rachel apologetically. "Hey, I didn't mean anything by it. He and Sam are just friends. Zeke seemed to miss having a family environment, so I was being friendly, but maybe he's found that since the last time we saw him."

I recalled a brief conversation with Zeke where he'd told me that I'd made the house feel more like a home, so I hoped that he had. Regardless, Cait seemed genuine in her reasons. Hopefully, Rachel could see that, then tell us how long this thing between them had been going on.

"I'm sorry," Rachel said, hiding her face behind her long hair.

Cait nudged herself between us, lifting Rachel's head up with one finger. "We've all been there and, if we haven't been, we will be soon. Love makes us do crazy things. No hard feelings over here."

Damn, Cait really was kind.

"Thank you," Rachel said, sounding a little more like herself.

"How about we get some drinks and see what kind of trouble we can get into?" Nikki suggested.

Cait and I were both shaking our heads. "I've had enough trouble to last me a lifetime," she said.

Oh, how I understood that.

CHAPTER 10

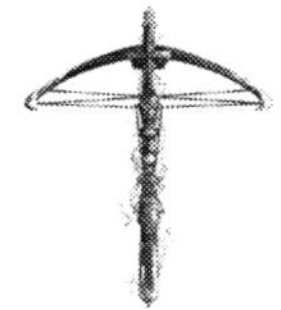

WE ENDED UP HAVING TWO DRINKS EACH BEFORE THE guys made it back. Cait went on to tell us about how she met Roman and almost walked away from him. A mistake she'd never repeat. Funny how I'd almost chosen not to trust Maciah. I found a lot about her story relatable.

When Maciah, Zeke, and Roman rejoined us, I was surprised to see Maciah smiling. Something good must have come from his meeting with the informant.

"What happened?" I asked as he wrapped an arm around me, kissing the side of my head.

"Not here. Just know things are finally looking up for us," he said.

"We're going to head out. We have a long few

days on the road," Roman said once he had Cait back in his arms.

Cait groaned while the rest of us girls laughed. The feeling of having friends was foreign to me. It had been so long since I'd let people in, but I couldn't deny it had been good for my soul. If I'd been facing Silas and Viktor on my own, I wasn't sure where I'd be right then.

Rachel eyed Zeke. Now that I knew there was something between them, I couldn't help but try to figure out what exactly that meant. Rachel wouldn't spill anything more than what Nikki had put together. She said it was too new and they didn't want to ruin the dynamic of the group if things didn't work out.

I understood why they were keeping things quiet, but it didn't mean I liked it.

Cait hugged each of us and held on to me a little longer, whispering in my ear. "Don't forget to call me if you need help. I texted you so you have my number."

"Thank you. I'll charge my phone as soon as I'm home." I hadn't even thought twice about it since before I was taken by Dmitri.

As they left the club, Maciah glanced around, seeming to look for someone.

"Is everything okay?" I asked.

He nodded. "Just checking on things. It's been a while since I've been here. We'll leave soon."

That was preferred. I wanted to know what they'd learned.

Zeke was watching Rachel. There was a slight grin on his face that he was trying to hide, but that wasn't happening. Then, I wondered if Maciah knew and, if he didn't, would he mind that two of his top vampires were hooking up?

"Did you see Bennett?" Zeke asked Maciah.

Nikki's attention rose. "Bennett is here?"

"We saw him on the way into the meeting, but I haven't caught sight of him since we came out of the private room," Zeke said.

Nikki frowned while Maciah still searched the room. This guy must have been the reason why we hadn't left yet.

"Who's Bennett?" I asked.

"He used to live at the nest with us. He had been around longer than any of us before he left a while back," Zeke answered.

"He's not here anymore. Let's get back to the house," Maciah said, grabbing my hand and heading toward the door without waiting for confirmation from anyone else.

I glanced behind us, and they were all following. Rachel had her arm around Nikki. Apparently, there was plenty to be talked about later.

The car was already waiting for us when we got outside. I didn't know how or why, but I rolled with it. The sooner we were within the confines of the vehicle, the sooner Maciah and Zeke could share what they learned.

Since I arrived at the Mercedes before Zeke, I stole the front seat. Not only because I wanted to be closer to Maciah while he filled us in, but I wanted to see if Rachel would sit next to Zeke in the backseat.

I watched as Nikki got in first, with Rachel next, followed by Zeke. At least that had worked out how I hoped. I wouldn't push Rachel and Zeke together, but I had no problem opening the door for them to grow closer. I would love nothing more than to see them happy. Together.

As soon as all of the doors were shut and Maciah had the car in drive, I turned to him. "Spill it, Vampire."

He laughed. "You can't call me that anymore now that you're one."

"Why not? You could call me the same," I said.

His eyes darkened as he slowly turned toward me. "There are plenty of other things I'd rather call you."

Nikki gagged. "Don't forget you're not alone in this car."

I smirked, not at all sorry.

"The informant is a vampire that likes to do

business with the highest bidder. We can't guarantee he won't tell Silas he spoke with us for more money, but it was a risk worth taking and paid off, regardless of what happens next," Maciah said.

"What did he say?" I asked eagerly.

Maciah grinned and met my gaze again. "Your blood didn't work for Silas."

A pit grew in my stomach. "Why? What was wrong with it?"

Sure, it was a good thing, but what did that say about me? My blood was supposed to be filled with original vampire power. Did that mean I wasn't going to be who everyone thought?

"I didn't ask many questions, but as soon as I heard that, I had a couple of theories. The first seeming most reasonable," Maciah said.

"And that would be?" I pressed when he didn't continue.

"You were still technically human when Silas took your blood. You had some vampire traits, but that didn't necessarily make you one. I believe that your blood didn't contain what Silas was looking for, but it does now that you've died and turned. The biggest question is, did Silas figure that out as well, or does he think you're useless to him now?"

His theory made sense, and I should have been happier Silas wasn't all powerful because of me, but the knot at my insides hadn't ceased growing. "What about your other theory?"

Maciah's grip tightened around the steering wheel. "That doesn't matter. It won't happen."

I settled my hand on his flexing arm. "We can't be sure of that. Especially if you keep me in the dark."

"You might have scared Silas with threats of Viktor before, making him willing to gamble with only taking your blood instead of you, but what if it wasn't enough? There's a chance that Silas needs to take every drop in your body for the consumption spell to work and give him the power he seeks," Maciah said without taking his eyes off the road.

We were all quiet as we considered that option. The one that meant Silas was still as big of a problem as before and that he would be back, regardless of what he had figured out.

"None of that matters. We'll go after him first. He's growing weaker as the days pass, right? And he really only had the upper hand on our land before because he took us by surprise. Let's do the same to him," I said.

"That's not as easy as it sounds. Even if we gather every vampire loyal to Maciah, we're still outnumbered three-to-one against the army Silas has built if we go to his nest," Zeke added.

I thought on that the rest of the drive home while everyone else stayed quiet. When we pulled into the driveway of the house, Maciah parked in the garage, and everyone seemed conflicted on what we'd learned. Some of it was good, some not so much. Either way, hope wasn't lost. There had to be something we could do.

"What about the wolves? Did you ask Roman for his help?" I asked as we headed inside.

Maciah nodded. "They'll join us when, or if, necessary, but I don't know if calling on that card so soon is best. We have no idea what to expect from Viktor."

Unfortunately, that made sense.

"It's late. Let's take a rest for the night and meet up again in the morning," Nikki suggested. There was a sadness in her eyes that I'd never seen before, and I assumed it had to do with the former nest member who had been at the club.

I wanted to find out who Bennett was to her and why he'd left, but before I could suggest just us girls hang out, Nikki blurred out of the room.

"She's right. We don't want to make any decisions too quickly without considering every aspect," Zeke said just before leaving as well.

Rachel waved and disappeared with the others.

Once we were alone, Maciah tossed me over his shoulder. "No more thinking for you tonight, either."

"Ha, good luck with that," I said while dangling upside down.

His hand squeezed my ass. "I don't need any luck."

Heat pooled in my core as I squeezed my legs together. Yeah, he really didn't.

Within seconds, we were in Maciah's room where I'd been staying most nights since becoming a vampire. My emotions had been too out of control to leave me alone for the first few days, and since sexual neediness was part of that, Maciah took night watch without question. It also helped that his room was magically sound-proofed.

He'd been caring, loving, and well-versed in my every need, knowing exactly how to release the frenzy that had been building inside me for days on end.

Every touch was purposeful and filled with passion like I'd never known. My skin shivered in anticipation that tonight would be no different than the past week. Maciah was never in a hurry. He reminded me daily that we had forever now. There was no race to pass the days or nights.

Maciah lay me on the bed before backing up to undo the buttons of his shirt. I reached forward, working on the charcoal belt that matched his fancy shoes.

As my fingers tugged at his zipper, Maciah dropped his shirt to the floor and nudged me back. "Patience."

That seemed to be his favorite speed.

He pulled my shirt over my head. "I don't want to dwell on what we learned, but I don't want to ignore how it might be affecting you, either. Are you okay?"

I wasn't sure how to answer his question. I was and I wasn't. There were too many uncertainties to be sure how things might affect us. Zeke had been right in suggesting we took the night to process what we'd learned.

"I'm good. Some time alone is exactly what we needed," I said confidently, reaching up to let my fingers trail down his chest.

He pulled me flush against him. "You're less anxious tonight. This is good."

My lips pressed against his chest. "I'm a fast learner."

Maciah was on top of me in the next moment—his vampire speed impressive and useful. He stroked my cheek with one hand and brushed my hair back with the other as he stared into my eyes.

The feelings between us were big. We'd yet to use words to describe how we felt, but they weren't needed when our actions were so much louder.

He kissed me once before leaning up to rid me of the pants plastered to my legs. I stretched my arms above my head and arched my back as he kissed around my belly button while his hands finished undressing me.

My eyes closed, soaking in the moment and the feelings Maciah evoked within me. My pulse quickened, my skin ached for his touch, and my core throbbed with a need only he could satisfy.

Maciah's sweet scent invaded my every sense, and I couldn't imagine where I would be if things had gone differently between us.

"I've got you," he whispered in my ear before nipping at my sensitive skin.

His hand slowly moved between us until his fingers rubbed over my center. I moaned for more of his talents and he didn't disappoint, using his touch to make me come and devouring my mouth with his tongue.

Even if we had this every night, I would never have enough of him.

Pressure was building inside me, and I began to tighten around his fingers, on the cusp of my release, only to have him pull his hand away from where I wanted it most. Before I could object, Maciah picked me up and had me pressed against the wall, entering me in one swift motion.

I screamed in pleasure and shock as he pounded into me relentlessly, holding me close and secure.

My head was tilted back, but he gripped the back of my hair, pushing my head forward until our eyes locked. His hips moved faster and there was nothing I could do but surrender to the wave of passion he'd created between us.

My core tightened around him again as my nails tore into his skin. Just as I hit my climax, he gripped my neck, holding me prisoner against him as my body turned into a writhing mess from his touch.

While I came down from the high, Maciah brought us back to the bed, not even close to done with me. It didn't matter that it was nearly three in the morning. We never tired of each other.

Until the sun was up, nothing else mattered except the two of us.

CHAPTER 11

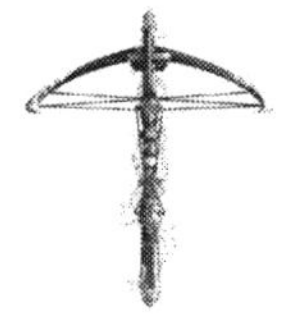

Our group met in Maciah's office the following morning. It was time to decide what to do with the information we learned about Silas, and I couldn't have been more eager. I knew what *I* wanted, but this vampire had been their nemesis for decades.

I'd gotten justice for my family twice in a row, first with Rigo and then Dmitri. Maciah and the others deserved the same sense of gratification I'd had while taking the lives of my family's murderers. Even though there was still one more out there, I knew Viktor's days were numbered. If we didn't find him first, he still had a debt to repay from someone above him. If Viktor didn't make his move soon, someone else would.

"So, I did a lot of thinking last night," Rachel said

as she entered the room with a tray of steaming mugs.

I sniffed the air. "Is that blood-laced coffee?"

She grinned at me. "Sure is."

"I think I love you," I murmured as I stole a cup from her. I took the first drink from my mug and nearly melted in my seat at how sweet yet dark the coffee tasted. It was unlike anything I'd ever had, and I knew exactly what I'd be making myself every morning when I got up.

She laughed. "That's a given. But seriously, I have an idea," she said while passing out the drinks.

"What's that?" Nikki asked.

I momentarily felt bad that I'd spent all night with Maciah instead of going to check on her, but we were a lot alike, and something told me time alone was what she'd needed most. Later, we'd have time to chat.

"I think Maciah's first theory is correct. Amersyn's blood was useless until she became a vampire. We need to tempt Silas with it and draw him out somewhere we stand a chance against him and whatever vampires he will bring with him," Rachel said.

"Maybe somewhere neutral where neither of us would technically have the advantage," Nikki added.

"Exactly. He's desperate, and people in his

predicament make stupid choices. We need to use that to our advantage," she added.

Maciah nodded his agreement, which surprised me. "I was thinking something similar. He has to be close still. I don't see him going far until he has what he wants."

"Drawing him out where he might not have all of his army with him is our best bet at beating him. Since Silas and Amersyn aren't linked, she will still be able to kill him, so we won't need outside help if we can lessen the vampires he has at his side," Zeke said.

"How are we going to draw him out?" Nikki asked.

"With me as the bait. Like Rachel said, we have to tempt him with what he needs," I said confidently.

"I don't think so," Maciah said, this time not surprising me.

"Take your protector hat off for a minute and think about it. Why else would Silas risk leaving his hideout? The only way to separate him from his army is by letting him think he has won. He knows how much I hate vampires. I've made that very clear to anyone I cross paths with. I can make him think I hate what I've become and I'm ready for it to be over," I said.

"But why would you go to him to die? He won't believe you, and if he knows it's a trap, then he'll bring more than enough help," Nikki said, making a valid point, but I was already prepared for that.

"I was taken from the one place I was supposed to be safest. I can convince him that I've parted ways from your nest, and this is my final 'eff you' to Maciah before I go out," I said, wincing a little as the words left my mouth. "Not that I blame any of you for my kidnapping, but it's a believable story."

Maciah's eyes darkened. I knew a part of him still held himself accountable for what happened to me, but at least the dying part was out of the way. Though, I was going to need to figure out how I died for real, so I could avoid that in the future. All I knew for sure was that anyone who wanted me dead for good was going to have to work a lot harder to kill me now that I was a vampire with original power running through my veins.

"Amersyn does make a good point. She has years of rage to pull from, and she won't be vulnerable. We can work on vampire fight training for a week or so before we act. With what she already knows, it won't take long to get her ready," Rachel said.

"And what if that doesn't work? What if Silas doesn't believe her and we're too late to stop him from killing her once things are in motion?" Maciah asked with a glower.

I reached for his hand, intertwining our fingers. "Nothing has to be decided today. Silas isn't coming for us tomorrow. We can think on this plan while considering others."

A deep rumble echoed from Maciah's chest, and I sighed. I knew he wouldn't like the plan, but with some more time to think about it, I knew he'd see reason. We didn't really have time to waver on what we were going to do, and he knew that. I'd only mentioned the idea of other options to hopefully make him feel a bit better about what was going to happen.

Nobody else said anything, so I let go of Maciah's hand and stood. "I need to go shower and punch some things."

"I'm needed here to handle some things I've been ignoring in the nest lately," Maciah said, ruining my plans of cracking some more tile in the shower with him.

Nikki stood next. "I could punch some things."

Rachel joined her. "Me, too."

"And I'm going to stay here," Zeke said with a smirk.

Perfect. Hopefully, Zeke would work on convincing Maciah that we had a solid plan already in place.

I pulled Maciah up from the couch and held his face between my hands. "Promise me you'll think about what I said. If you still hate the idea by the time I come back, then give us a plan B."

He pressed his head against mine. “I promise to try to keep an open mind.”

I gave him a quick kiss before meeting Rachel and Nikki at the door. Once we were in the hallway, Rachel threw an arm around me. “I’m so proud of you.”

I laughed. “Thanks. Why?”

“Because you’re all calm and collected and kicking ass at this whole vampire thing,” she said.

Nikki nudged my other side. “Rach is right. You have a handle on your thirst and emotions most newborns don’t until months after they’ve turned. Sure, they aren’t locked up after a couple weeks, but there is still constant internal struggle they often deal with. As of two days ago, I don’t see any of that from you.”

I shrugged, feeling awkward from the praise. “It’s probably just because I’m an heir.”

“Or it’s because you’re just that determined. State of mind has a lot to do with how quickly vampires acclimate,” Nikki added.

I remembered right after I’d become a vampire. I was so thirsty, but I refused to be a murderer. Maybe she had a point.

We went into my room, and I had intended to take a shower, but since they followed me and got comfortable on my bed, I figured this was the time we could all catch up on the things we didn't talk about in front of Maciah and Zeke. Men didn't need to know everything, especially when it had to do with them.

The thought of Cait from the night before made me remember it had been much too long since I checked my phone. Given I'd been busy mastering all things vampire, keeping up with the outside world hadn't been at the top of my priority list.

My phone was dead on my dresser, so I plugged it in before going to sit on the bed with Rachel and Nikki. "So, who's going first?" I asked.

Nikki laughed. "What do you mean?"

"Okay, fine. I'll go. I'm having sex with Maciah," I said with hushed tones as if it was a big secret.

Rachel gasped. "Out of wedlock? How scandalous of you!"

She really was a great friend who had done a good job of pushing me outside of my comfort zones. It had taken me a while to be grateful for that, but I wouldn't ever forget her efforts.

"I'm shamelessly shameful," I said with a wicked grin.

"I can only agree to that statement if you answer one question," Nikki said, pausing for dramatic effect. "Is he as commanding behind closed doors as he is outside them?"

The image of him slamming me against the wall

entered my mind, and I bit my lip just thinking about it as chills raced along my exposed skin.

Nikki fanned her face. "Enough said."

"Nothing more has happened with me and Zeke, so if you're expecting juicy details, I have none. Like I said, we're being cautious and taking time to get to know each other better under different circumstances," Rachel said.

Her words didn't surprise me. She was a naturally happy person, but I was certain the idea of putting her feelings out there wasn't the easiest when they made her vulnerable. Zeke had better be kind to her or I was going to remind him of how it felt to be stabbed by me again.

I eyed Nikki next, and she threw her hands in the air. "What? I don't have a secret lover."

"No, but who's Bennett?" I asked.

Her eyes darkened and I felt bad for bringing him up, but if we ran into him, I wanted to be prepared with whatever information was available.

"Bennett is the first and only man I've dated since becoming a vampire. It never felt right before. My husband might believe I'm dead, but I know differently. Technically, I'm still married. It wasn't until I met Bennett that I even considered moving on. He was everything my husband wasn't, which kept me from comparing the two men. But Bennett had a very different introduction to the vampire world than the rest of us did," Nikki said.

Rachel nodded. "Silas is evil, but there are worse than him out there. They're just not as greedy, so they stay under the radar for the most part."

"What happened to Bennett?" I asked.

"After five years of being together, I never got the whole story, but I do know that he went through a bloodlust decade where no one was off limits," Nikki answered.

A whole decade? So many innocent lives lost. The thought made fury swirl within me, but this conversation wasn't about me and my drive to stop vampires from killing people. It was about Nikki and Bennett, who at some point had to have changed, so I tucked my own thoughts away.

"Obviously, he stopped being a psychopath if he lived here. Why did he leave?" I asked next. To me, that was more important than his past. If Bennett had gone back to his old ways, he just might be at the top of my list of vampires to kill after Silas and Viktor.

Nikki teared up as she spoke. "We were out together, away from the nest, and someone from his past showed up. I got hurt pretty badly, but it was nothing vampire healing couldn't take care of. Bennett wouldn't look at me for days after I was better. I tried reaching out to him in various ways, but every attempt was ignored.

"One morning, I woke up to find a letter on my pillow. He apologized for what happened to me and promised nothing would ever hurt me again because of him. He was leaving and never coming back, because that's what he thought was best for everyone. I didn't believe he was even still in the area until last night."

Damn, that was rough. On one hand, I could understand Bennett's perspective, but on the other, he had no right to take the blame like he had. In the end, he'd hurt Nikki more than anything from his past probably could have.

I leaned across the bed and gave her a hug. "I'm sorry that happened, but maybe him being back means he's ready to apologize again. This time for being an idiot."

She snorted through her tears. "I doubt it. I'm sure we'll never see him again. I don't even know why I'm so upset. It's been almost four years since I've seen him."

"Love doesn't cease to exist just because the recipient goes away," Rachel said.

Wasn't that the truth. No matter what kind of love it was. Seven years later and I knew without a doubt that the love I had for my own family had only continued to grow.

"I think that's enough sharing for the day, unless anyone has anything they want to get off their chest?" I offered, but nobody spoke up. "How about we go beat the hell out of each other in the gym, then?"

"Yes, please," Nikki sighed and got up.

"I'm going to take a quick shower and meet you ladies down there," I said, leaping off the bed.

Rachel scrunched her nose. "Why wouldn't you just take one after?"

"If you've never taken a scalding hot shower to loosen up your muscles before a workout, then you've been missing out on a lot of awesomeness."

"We'll have to take your word for it," Nikki said as they left my room.

Crazy vampires didn't know what they were missing.

I headed into the bathroom and turned on the shower. While I waited for the water to heat up, I went to my closet and got my clothes sorted.

On my way back to the bathroom, the vibration of my phone caught my attention. I went to pick it up and was shocked to see all of the texts and voicemails.

Maciah: Why aren't you answering your phone?

Maciah: Amersyn??

Maciah: I'm going to burn every city down until I find you.

Those were from right after I'd been taken by Dmitri. Maciah always said such sweet things.

Dave: We should meet again soon.

Dave: Why aren't you answering?

Dave: Something isn't right. We need to talk.

In between those texts from Dave were a dozen voicemails from him that I wasn't looking forward to listening to. He was turning into a mother hen. I needed to make sure he knew I had things handled.

As I kept scrolling, there were notifications from my hunter app and more voicemails from unknown numbers until I finally got to the more recent stuff, and the messages had my ire building by the word.

Steve: Dave's missing, Amersyn. He needed you and you weren't there. What the hell is going on?

Dave: I have your bartender. - Silas

Mother effing effer.

CHAPTER 12

STEAM ROLLED OUT OF THE BATHROOM AS I STOOD THERE staring at my phone. Silas had Dave. A human who had nothing to do with what was happening. A human that I wasn't supposed to care about. A human who shouldn't have been on Silas's radar, and I knew just who to blame.

Simon.

The slimy rat of a hunter had to have done this. He was working with Viktor. I knew that from the information Dave had given me before. I was also aware it was completely possible for Silas and Viktor to be working together, one hoping to screw over the other once they got their hands on me, just like Dmitri had intended.

It was all starting to make sense, and I now had a

hunter I desperately wanted to murder alongside the vampires.

I read the messages again, then began listening to the voicemails. Each one was more frantic than the last.

My phone had been long forgotten until last night. Silas's message was from just a few hours after we got back from Nyx, which hopefully meant he hadn't had Dave for long.

I was nearly done listening to the messages in my voicemail when Maciah walked into my room. "What's wrong?" he asked immediately.

"Throw out every plan we thought we had. We're going after Silas. Now." My voice was clipped as Dave's distressed message echoed through my ear.

"Why? What happened?"

"Silas has Dave. I don't care if we're being set up. I have to get him back. I won't let him die because of me," I said as the last message ended, then tossed Maciah my phone. "Read the texts. Listen to the voicemails. We can't let Silas kill him."

Maciah began scrolling through my phone, and I could sense his frustrations rising just like mine had as he continued.

"We're going to figure this out. Your bartender will be fine," Maciah said as he pulled me into his arms.

I pushed him away with the smallest amount of

effort, not trying to be rude, but comfort wasn't what I needed when I was furious like this.

"We have to call Dave's phone and see if Silas answers," I said as Rachel and Nikki walked in.

"Who's Dave?" Nikki asked.

"The hot bartender from Crossroads," Rachel answered. "Why would Silas answer his phone?"

I took my phone from Maciah, and handed it to Nikki's waiting hand, letting them see what I had.

"What are we doing about this?" Nikki asked.

Maciah ran a hand through his hair while the other took the phone back from Nikki. "I'm not sure, but we can't do anything without thinking it through first. Hasty decisions will only get Dave killed."

I snarled and flexed my fists at my side, even though he was probably right.

Maciah reached for me, lifting my chin until he had my full attention. "I promise to take this seriously, but you're too closely involved. Let me figure something out. Go workout with Rachel and Nikki, since that's what you were about to do anyway. I will come get you as soon as I have more information. Maybe we can still use your plan to help make this easier. We'd just have to skip the week of preparation."

"Skip whatever we have to. We need to do something tonight, Maciah." I wouldn't leave Dave with that power-hungry vampire any longer than we had to. "And I'm going to need my phone. I need to let Steve know I didn't disappear and that we're working on things," I added.

"Who's Steve?" Maciah asked.

"Dave's boyfriend who knows about the supernatural world, but he has nothing to do with it other than picking Dave up from Crossroads. We won't involve him. I just..." I didn't know what I wanted, but doing something as simple as responding to Steve seemed like a good start to all of this craziness.

Maciah handed me my phone, then grabbed my shoulders, giving me a slight shake. "It's going to be fine."

Damn, I sure hoped so.

He kissed my forehead and left my room. I took several deep breaths to get a hold on the elevated rage I was feeling. If this had happened a few days ago, I would have sped out of this mansion and given Silas whatever he wanted.

As much as I still wanted to do that, I knew Maciah was right. Silas wasn't going to kill Dave yet. As long as my bartender was still useful to the vampire, then we had time.

Nikki stepped closer, her expression serious. "What can we do?"

I had no answer for her. Instead, I found Steve's number and brought the phone to my ear. With every ring, my stomach churned with thoughts of what could be happening to Dave as we stood there.

This was why I didn't want friends before. The guilt that was building was a pretty crappy feeling.

"Amersyn?" Steve's voice was frantic.

"I got your message. I know where Dave is," I said first before he could go off on me for ghosting them.

He let out a sputtered sigh. "Oh, thank God. When will he be home?"

"I don't know." Then again, I really hadn't thought through how I was going to handle this call.

"What do you mean? If you know where he is, bring him back to me, Amersyn."

"What I mean is that you know the kind of world we work in. You knew the dangers of Dave's job. I'm going to do whatever I can to get him, but nothing about this situation is simple."

Steve let out a small cry. "Those vampires he's been going on about have him, don't they? I told him to quit, but he promised he would be okay. He believed you'd protect him. Where have you been all this time?" His tone was accusing and rightly so. I never made promises to Dave, but he knew what I stood for. He had trust in me, and Steve knew that.

"I haven't had my phone for a while."

"If you had, maybe none of this would have happened," Steve snapped.

He was upset, and I was the easiest person to blame. I knew that, but it didn't stop me from feeling like the biggest piece of trash on earth.

"Talking to you isn't going to solve anything. I have to go. I'll let you know as soon as I have him," I said. If I didn't get off the phone with Steve soon, I was going to do something stupid.

My thumb hovered over the end button as Steve called out. "I have something that might help."

"What's that?" I asked.

"Dave told me that vampires have been grouping together at the bar. They sit in the corners, watching everyone else, waiting for something. Another hunter has been working with them. Dave said his name is Simon. He wanted to tell you that you couldn't trust the hunters and needed to stay away from Crossroads."

Yeah, unfortunately, those were already things I assumed or knew. Steve had just confirmed them.

"Thanks, Steve. I'll get Dave back for you as soon as I can," I said and hung up.

As I turned around, Rachel and Nikki were standing there, concern lacing their features. Rachel held a mug out to me. "I got this for you."

I shook my head. I didn't want sustenance. I wanted heads on a platter.

"It's a good idea. We all need to drink more than

usual today if we're going to be fighting tonight," Nikki added.

This was not the fight I had planned on. It was supposed to be simple. I was going to lure Silas somewhere we could have the upper hand. Now, he was going to be able to do the same to me.

I wanted to scream and rage. I wanted to kill every vampire that didn't live in this nest.

Rachel nudged the blood closer to me. "Maciah is going to figure something out."

He had better, because all I could see was red. He was right. I was too close to see anything else, and that was what Silas was counting on. The bastard was hoping I'd act recklessly to give him the advantage, but I wasn't the same hunter I'd been a month ago.

Whatever Simon had told those vampires about me no longer applied. Not even my strengths.

"Do you think they know I'm a vampire?" I asked them.

"It's possible. We haven't heard anything, but that doesn't mean much with how busy we've been," Nikki answered.

That was something we needed to figure out. I wanted to call Silas myself and bait him, see what he knew, but I was going to wait for Maciah. We were supposed to be a team, and I trusted he was doing whatever he could to figure out the best play.

"How about we go to the gym like we planned? It would be a good way to let out some aggressions," Rachel suggested.

Mention of our workout reminded me that I hadn't even turned off my shower, so I went to the bathroom to do so. The place was a sauna. After I shut the water off, I leaned against the wall and closed my eyes.

How could we best Silas without Dave getting hurt in the process?

I really wanted to blow the vampire's safehouses up and call it a day, but that wasn't an option we could consider without killing people who didn't deserve to die, like Dave.

Given I hadn't done any real training yet with my new abilities, I decided Rachel was right and that the gym might be the best place for me, so I pushed off the wall and went back to my bedroom. I took the mug from her and downed the contents in one go.

"Let me change, and then we can go," I said before turning toward my closet.

"She's all yours," I heard Rachel say to Nikki.

I smirked as I began undressing and searching for my gym clothes. I was going to do some damage during our workout, but I'd keep myself in check, making sure my hits wouldn't be anything that a vampire couldn't quickly recover from.

Another minute later, I had my hair in a braid and

was ready to walk out the door. Rachel and Nikki had been right. I was already feeling better after another dose of blood, but that didn't mean my underlying ire was forgotten. I'd use those emotions to push every boundary I could to make sure that nothing went wrong when we found Silas.

I tucked my phone into the side pocket of my workout pants, and we headed down the hallway. When we were halfway there, an idea hit me. I grabbed both of their arms, halting their movements. "What about my special ability? The additional mind control stuff? How do we work on drawing that out?"

Rachel frowned. "I don't know. I mentioned it to Zeke, but he told me that he and Maciah weren't sure either. They suspected any special abilities would surface on their own, but I can do some digging to see if they're right. I know every section of the library. I can go there while the two of you beat the hell out of each other."

She seemed pretty happy with that idea, and I had no objections, so I nodded. "Go for it. Come get us as soon as you find something. If Maciah has something sooner, we'll find you first."

She disappeared in a blur, and I turned to Nikki. "She doesn't like the fighting much, even though she's good at it."

"No, she doesn't. Rachel wants to believe the best

in everyone. It's what makes her more human than any of us, but that doesn't mean she won't tear heads off when needed. Her ability to balance her badassness is why I love her," Nikki answered with a smirk as we continued toward the gym.

I laughed. "Her persistence also makes it hard not to adore her."

We got to the gym that took up nearly the entire sublevel floor of the mansion. I'd worked out in there many times since my arrival, but seeing the place with my vampire eyes gave me a new sense of appreciation for the set up.

Everything was spaced out. The walls were padded, so they hopefully wouldn't crack when someone slammed into them. The floor even had some give to it that I hadn't noticed before.

The biggest plus was that I could feel the air circulation that kept not only the smell of sweat to a minimum, but the temperature down. I used to hate that, but understood better now with my new body.

"Ready to be distracted for as long as it takes to figure out a plan?" Nikki asked as other vampires began to turn our way.

I nodded. I counted eight others in the room, all working out separately. "As long as you're prepared for the beating that I'm ready to hand out," I joked. Mostly.

She chuckled. "Let's see about that."

I followed Nikki to the far-left corner where nobody was. There were extra mats on the floor and various weapons scattered around. I hadn't been over in this area much, really only using the exercise equipment and some of the sparring mats when someone was willing to go up against me before.

I took my shirt off, choosing to work out in my sports bra and yoga pants, then set my phone on top of my shirt out of the way. As soon as my foot stepped within the designated circle, I had the wind knocked out of me and I was on my ass.

"Vampire fighting, lesson one: Always be prepared. No matter where you are or who you're with, you can't ever be too cautious," Nikki said as she mounted me.

I shoved my palm into her chest and got to my feet as she landed on hers. "Lesson received."

We circled each other twice before I made my first move, lunging for the vampire and missing by inches.

"Lesson two: Never throw the first punch. Something you should have known even as a hunter." She tsked at me and I sneered, because she was right.

I took a better look at my surroundings, needing to find a way to get my hands on Nikki. She was fast, but so was I. I just had to get a better understanding of how to use that speed to my advantage, along with all of the other skills I'd acquired over the years.

There was a rope behind her, and an idea came to me. I feigned right and left before going right. I darted around Nikki, swooped up the rope and wrapped both ends around my hands as I used the wall behind us for momentum.

I kicked off the cushioned surface, not getting as much umph as I'd hoped for, but it was good enough to get where I needed, which was right behind Nikki.

Using my leg, I swept hers out from under her and brought the rope over her neck, pulling her flush against me until her windpipe started to be crushed.

She tapped my hand, choking for air as I let go. "Lesson three: Use whatever is at your disposal to win," she rasped.

Nikki might have had her lessons, but I trusted my instincts. Those were what I needed to get Dave back and kill Silas. He wouldn't get away again.

I only had to remember who I was as a hunter and learn how to meld those abilities with who I was as a vampire. I didn't have to choose between who I was in my old life and who I was becoming in the new one I'd been thrown into.

I'd find a way to be both. More importantly, I'd show these vampires they couldn't hurt the people I cared about and live to tell the story.

CHAPTER 13

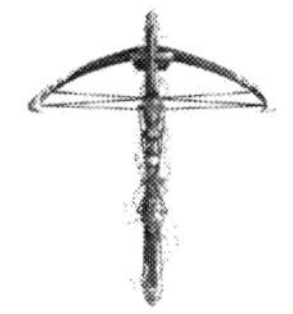

Nikki continued with her "lessons", and I soaked every one of them up as we exchanged blows. She was a solid opponent, and I was glad we'd had this alone time. We didn't talk much between fighting, but I already felt closer to her.

"Again?" she asked, breathing hard just like me.

"I'd love to say yes, but we should check on Rachel. I was hoping she'd have found something by now," I said.

Nikki tensed. "So was I, but don't bother going to her. Last time I tried to interrupt her while she was watching videos on how to crochet, she nearly tore out my eyes. Girl does not like to be disrupted when she's on a mission."

I shook my head with a smirk. "Good to know."

Nikki took a seat on the mats, leaning back on her

elbows. She let out a heavy sigh as I joined her. "Are you doing okay?" I asked.

"It's almost my son's fiftieth birthday." She chuckled darkly. "Crazy to think I have a son who is twice the age that I look."

I hated to pry, but she'd opened the door and, if she wanted to talk, then I had no problem being there for her. "Have you seen him since?" I asked.

She shrugged. "Here and there. I check in at least once a year, or when I'm having a really bad day. It's better not to see them. Christopher, my son, he was so young when I was turned, but I'm still afraid he'll recognize me from pictures I'm sure he's seen. Even if he thinks I'm just an uncanny lookalike, I don't want to confuse him by getting too close."

"What about your husband? Did you ever think about reaching out to him after Maciah saved you?" I asked.

"Every day. He'd probably understand even, but how fair would that be to him? I'd never wish this life on anyone, and it's not exactly safe for humans to be close to us. On top of that, I'm selfish. I couldn't stand to be close to him, knowing he was going to die or be turned into a monster like I thought I was. By the time I accepted that vampires didn't have to be evil, my husband was moving on with his life. I didn't fault him for that, and I didn't want to disrupt his world all over again."

I couldn't imagine being in her position, but I could see the rationale in how she'd handled things. I couldn't say I'd have done them any differently, but then again, one never knows how they'll truly do something until they're forced to. Hell, I'd thought I would kill myself once I became a vampire and nothing of the sort was a consideration now.

"If you ever want someone to join you when you go visit them next time that won't ask questions, know that I'm always happy to go with you," I offered.

She smiled, but it was forced. "I appreciate that. What about you? Any family left after what happened to you?"

"No. Not that I know of anyway. My mother had kept my father from me, so maybe there was more, but as far as I'm aware, my parents were only children with single moms who died early. One from drugs, the other cancer. Being human isn't much safer than hanging around vampires, I guess."

Nikki grunted. "Possibly. How did you go from orphan to hunter?" she asked.

Ahhh, this wasn't exactly the conversation I wanted to have. Not because I didn't trust Nikki, but because it was still painful. Mostly because I'd been naïve, but also because my heart had been broken.

"You don't have to tell me if you don't want to," Nikki said when I didn't answer right away.

I could accept her offer to remain silent, but then a thought occurred to me that never had before. If I kept my past to myself, then that meant Caleb still had power over me. If I was too afraid to talk about him, that only made me weaker. Screw that.

"I was on the run from Child Protective Services. They wanted to place me in a group home until I was eighteen and could legally manage my inheritance, which was millions of dollars I never knew existed until I was on my own. Now that I know who my birth father was, I assume the money came from Darius and my mom hid it from my dad."

"She sounds like a smart woman," Nikki said with a small grin.

"She really was. Though, knowing my dad, he never would have taken advantage. The hiding of it was probably only to prevent questions being asked that she couldn't answer."

"Makes sense. What about the group homes?"

I shuddered, remembering those early days of grief. "I'd only spent one night in a group home, and I'd known immediately that I couldn't do it another. I was angry and confused. Monsters had killed my family, and the more time I had to process that fact, the more I knew that I had to find people who were aware of the monsters out in the world."

Nikki raised a brow. "Now, this I need to know.

How does a human teenager find those kinds of people?"

I laughed. "The internet of all places. Long story short, I made a connection with this guy named Caleb. He had a similar story to mine. Vampires killed his family and he vowed to destroy any he could find. When he found out I was living on the streets, he offered to give me a place to stay and to train me."

Nikki grimaced. "That sounds like the beginning of a great love story, or a horror movie."

"In all honesty, maybe a bit of both? It was good in the beginning. For the first year, I was as happy as I could get while grieving my family. Caleb never pushed me for anything. Only gave me a purpose to channel my rage into," I said, pausing as more memories that I'd kept locked away began to free themselves.

I was already feeling lighter, and I'd hardly told Nikki anything. For so many years, I'd kept this part of my life a secret, letting it fester inside me. I wished I'd found people like Nikki and Rachel long ago, or at least trusted that they could exist.

"What changed?" Nikki asked, prompting me to continue.

"I turned sixteen and decided to get emancipated through the courts, so I could get access to my inheritance. I had a home, a job, and I could care for myself. All thanks to Caleb. Waiting until I was eighteen and staying somewhat on the run seemed ridiculous. As soon as I made all of that happen, Caleb changed. He grew more controlling. Now that I look back, he was probably afraid of me leaving, but if he'd only treated me the same as he always had, I'd have stayed forever."

Nikki reached for my knee, giving it a soft squeeze. "Men aren't always the smartest when they're scared, as you've seen even with Maciah."

I nodded. Though, there was no comparing Caleb and Maciah. They were completely different men, and I was thankful for that.

I set my hand on top of Nikki's. "Thank you. I didn't know how much I needed to get some of that off my chest."

"That's what friends are for. Just don't tell Rachel she missed out on this. She'll be furious with us." Nikki laughed and I joined her.

Now that I'd told the story once, I had no problem filling Rachel in as well. Maybe the more I talked about the past, the more I could enjoy my future.

I glanced at the clock on the wall. It wasn't even eleven in the morning yet, and we'd already been in the gym for a few hours. I wanted nothing more than to reach out to Silas and figure out how he was going to play this, but it was best for me if we waited until nightfall to rescue Dave. Which meant the rest of the day was going to drag in the worst way.

The door to the gym opened and I spun around, hopeful it was Rachel. Instead, it was Maciah and Zeke. I tried not to let my disappointment show, but I knew I failed when Maciah's brow creased and Zeke grinned.

He clasped Maciah's shoulder. "Trouble in paradise already. That's not good."

Maciah shoved him away with little effort. "What's wrong?" he asked me.

"Nothing. We were expecting Rachel, but seeing you is good, too," I said, hopeful they'd learned something if they were here.

"I need your phone," he said.

"We're going to text Silas back," Zeke added.

My phone was still with my shirt, out of the way. I considered handing it over, but once Zeke mentioned they were going to send the text, I wanted to be part of it. The training with Nikki had taken the edge off my fury, and I had a better handle on my emotions.

"I can help with the message especially since it's supposed to be from me," I said.

"I'm not sure that's a good idea," Maciah said.

Nikki stepped to my side. "She's doing fantastic, Maciah. She handled the rage like a decades-old vampire and hasn't overreacted once since we got into the gym. I can't say that she'll stay that way if you hold her back."

Damn, I wasn't expecting her to talk to Maciah like that. I waited for his reprimand, but none came, which shocked me even more than Nikki's words.

"You're right." Maciah gave me his full attention. "You are doing better than any of us ever expected. I'm used to doing things my way, but I know this isn't just about me anymore. I want Silas dead, but he has your friend."

Warmth filled my chest at Maciah's words. I believed every one of them and didn't hesitate to turn and grab my phone.

I checked the screen before handing it over, hoping there would be a new message, but Silas was playing things cool. He'd only sent the one text and was waiting for us to show our hand. Frustrating, but not unexpected from the old bloodsucker.

Maciah glanced around the gym. "Let's go back to my office."

I nodded. There were even more vampires around the room, and we didn't need to provide them with a show. They'd know what they needed to when the time was right. Until then, I didn't trust many of them, not after knowing a guard had betrayed Maciah, getting me captured by Dmitri. Though it had worked out, it might not have, and I hoped to get my hands on that slimy vampire guard one day.

I reached for Maciah's hand, and we sped out of the room together, with Nikki and Zeke right behind us. In seconds, we were in his office, and I grinned. "I don't think that will ever get old."

"What?" Zeke asked.

"Going from point A to point B in the blink of an eye," I said, taking a seat on the couch.

Nikki joined me. "I still enjoy it. Besides drinking blood to survive, being a vamp isn't that bad of a deal when you're surrounded by the right people."

I nudged her. "Are you getting soft on me?"

She scoffed. "Hardly. I just kicked your ass several times over."

"Right. I'll let you stick with that story." I chuckled, then turned to Maciah because Dave wasn't far from my mind. "What's your plan?" I asked him.

He had my phone in his hand, turning it over and over as he thought. "I think we need to pretend you don't care about Dave. Make that the reason you took so long to respond."

I winced. "What if Silas sucks him dry, thinking Dave is no longer useful?"

"That's a risk, but you had rules before. Very specific ones that Simon would have known about, right?" Maciah asked.

"I did, but I wasn't a heartless hunter, either," I replied.

"We know that, and Simon might have said as much, but Silas isn't going to blindly believe that traitor. Anyone who would turn on their own kind isn't worthy to Silas. He might be a bastard, but he has standards, and loyalty means a lot to him," Maciah said.

I let his words sink in. "Then, wouldn't my lack of loyalty to Dave be a bad thing?"

"I asked the same thing when Maciah suggested this plan," Zeke said. "We are going off the fact that Silas won't be trusting Simon's word as law. You made a name for yourself as a hunter by killing more than your fair share of vampires over the years. Never once was it known that you worked with other people. So, why would Silas have any reason to believe that you truly care for Dave more than using him for good drinks and information from the patrons of the bar he happens to work at? Especially when you've already ignored his texts so far."

Zeke made a damn good point. That was exactly how I'd tried to treat Dave, because I didn't ever want him to be a target, so it shouldn't be a problem to get Silas to believe the same.

"What do you think Silas will do with that information?" Nikki asked.

"I've known Silas for a long time. I've tracked his moves and learned how he enjoys doing business. He has only ever cared about becoming more powerful than the next vampire. There's a small chance that he'll dispose of Dave, but Silas is more likely to hold on to the bartender for future use, like calling your bluff."

I felt sick to my stomach as soon as Maciah mentioned Dave being disposed of. My head was shaking before I could even get the words out. "This plan won't work. I understand why you think it's solid, but it's too much risk. I can't do this."

"Why not?" Maciah asked.

"I won't gamble with Dave's life based on what we think we know about Silas. He's desperate for my blood, knowing that Viktor could kill me at any moment. That means Silas may not make all the same choices he normally would. I gave Steve my word that I would bring Dave back, and I plan to do just that in the safest way possible," I said.

"What way could be safe enough for a human?" Zeke asked.

I got up and paced the room for a moment. We all had good ideas. Even the ones thought up before we knew Dave had been taken. There had to be an option that allowed us to keep control of the situation without putting Dave at risk.

"Silas might be dying, but he's not stupid. He will be able to sense my emotions the moment we're in his presence, so I can't pretend not to care about Dave, but I could play my feelings lightly. I need to be the one to call Silas. Not text him. He needs to know that I want Dave's life spared, but that I'm not playing his games, either. I have something Silas needs, and I'll convince him that it's not the end of my world if the bartender dies," I said, feeling good about the direction my thoughts were headed.

"But it will be the end of Silas's life if he doesn't get your blood," Nikki added.

I grinned. "Exactly. Silas needs my blood too badly. It doesn't matter how many hostages he attempts to take; I still hold the power. He will die without me, and I can even use the angle of wanting to end this vampire existence to draw him out. Ask for an exchange, Dave's life for mine. My final good deed before I go out."

Rachel burst into the room like the ray of sunshine she was and a book in her hand. "I got it!"

"Got what?" Maciah asked.

"She was in the library searching for something about how we can figure out what Amersyn's additional ability might be," Nikki said as Rachel plopped down next to me.

"Look at this right here," Rachel said, pointing to a paragraph of faded text.

I frowned. "I can see it, but I doubt I'll be able to read it."

She shushed me and took the book back to read it out loud herself. "Original vampires were created with the ultimate power to suit their personalities. Their heirs will receive the same, but the power won't be revealed until they've ended their human life and bonded to their protector. Once an ability has been triggered, the heir and his protector will always be connected as power breeds greed, and we cannot allow our heirs to succumb to the evil they will undoubtedly be tempted with."

I held a finger up. "Um, question. If all heirs before me were male, how does one bond with their protector?"

I'd already had sex with Maciah. I wasn't sure how much closer we could get.

"You have to bite each other," Rachel said nonchalantly.

My eyes widened. "I don't think I heard you right."

"Fang yes, you did. Sharpen those incisors, Am. You get to bite Maciah."

CHAPTER 14

My head started shaking slowly, the movements increasing with every turn until Maciah was in front of me, holding me still.

"Take a breath. It's not that big of a deal," he said softly.

I narrowed my eyes at him. "Says the person who has bitten other people before."

"You won't hurt me if that's what concerns you," he added.

I huffed in frustration. "I'm not worried about hurting you, Maciah, but what if I bite you and I don't want to stop there? I fought so hard to keep from hurting *anyone* right after I was turned. I never thought I would bite a single person—human or vampire. I thought that I could be stronger than these primal urges. Believing in that is the only thing that has kept me okay with all of this so far."

It was also possible that reality hadn't truly set in for me, and that I was still in a bit of denial, but after drinking glass after glass of blood, I figured I was past that point. This, though? Biting someone, even if it was only Maciah, didn't seem like something to be taken lightly.

"You have done better than any other vampire I've ever watched over. Your will is solid, and I don't have any worries that one bite will change what your heart so strongly believes," he said, staring me in the eyes and calming me with every word.

Maciah might have been right, but I needed a minute. I hadn't expected Rachel to say anything about biting. The shock wasn't easy to shake, especially knowing they were all counting on me to be okay with this.

I closed my eyes for a moment, remembering who I was and what I wanted. Blood would never truly rule me. Just because I needed the crimson liquid to survive didn't mean it controlled me.

I was more than a vampire. I was still Amersyn Holt. I would still hunt vampires and decide how I lived. Things were different now, but being turned hadn't changed who I was at the core.

My newly erratic emotions sometimes made it hard to remember those things, but I had people around me who weren't afraid to force me to take a moment and ground myself.

I opened my eyes again to find Maciah still holding my gaze with dark eyes. "Thank you," I murmured.

"Always."

"So, once I bite Maciah, I'm supposed to be able to do something like mind control that I can use against Silas?" I asked to whoever wanted to answer.

Maciah moved to sit next to me. "Mind control is a little different from what I think you'll have. Darius had compulsion, so it would make sense for that to be your ability as well."

"What's the difference? Both control the mind, right?" I asked.

"For vampires, compulsion can only be used on one person at a time, but mind control can be done on a group of people all at once. It takes the most powerful of our kind to wield that ability successfully. Only the eldest original vampire had been able to do that before," Zeke answered this time.

I wasn't keen on being able to force people to do things, but if it gave us a leg up against Silas, then I would do whatever it took to master the ability. We had to get Dave back alive. Anything less wasn't acceptable.

"As soon as Amersyn feels comfortable with her

ability, then we can contact Silas and arrange a meeting, but we shouldn't do so before in case he forces our hand before we're ready," Rachel said.

"The meeting is going to be a set-up," Nikki stated.

"As long as we know that walking in, then there's no point in worrying about it. We don't have a choice in facing him. Even if he didn't have the bartender, this is still a chance for us to draw him out," Zeke said.

"Amersyn and I need some time alone to discuss how this is going to work. We can hold off on specifics for the plan until we know where we're meeting Silas. Can one of you search for a location that is neutral to both vampire nests and preferably not close to where humans will be? We don't know how far Silas intends to take this," Maciah said.

"I'll also prepare the other vampires. Make sure they're ready to leave at a moment's notice," Zeke replied before heading out of the office.

"Do you need anything before we go?" Nikki asked me as she and Rachel stood.

"I'm good. Thank you both for your help this morning." Even though Rachel hadn't worked out with us, she'd found the answer we were looking for.

They both nodded at me and disappeared out of the door.

I was suddenly more nervous to be alone with

Maciah than I was the first time I stayed in his bed. Except I knew that was ridiculous. Maciah was safe. He wasn't going to force me to do anything I wasn't comfortable with. I trusted him explicitly.

"How are you handling all of this right now?" he asked me, taking my hand in his.

Our fingers melded together, and his warmth went straight to my chest, strengthening the connection I already felt with him. Everything was working out exactly how it was supposed to. I knew that, even if I didn't like it all the time.

I might have been the only female heir ever created, but I knew in my soul that it was because I was strong enough to handle whatever was headed toward us. So long as I continued trusting those at my side.

"I'm not looking forward to biting you, but I'm okay. I know my mind is probably making it out to be worse than it really is."

He squeezed my hand tighter. "I know you, Amersyn. There isn't anything you can't conquer once you set your mind to it."

"Thank you for believing in me and pushing me to be someone I didn't think I was capable of being," I said and truly meant the words. Bond or not, I'd known the minute Maciah appeared in my bedroom that he was going to be different. That he would somehow change my world.

"Do you want to talk about the biting now or wait until you've had some time to process?" he asked.

"Now. We don't have the luxury of time on our side. Dave needs me, and my vampire emotions will only get more intense, the longer I dwell on this," I said, sitting up straighter and facing him.

There wasn't any part of me that wanted to sink my teeth into Maciah's flesh. His blood didn't call to me like the humans' blood I'd scented in LA. He smelled divine with the citrus and vanilla wafting off him, but that was all sexual and nothing more.

I wasn't sure how I was going to do this, but I knew I had to try. If I didn't do everything I could to ensure we beat Silas and brought Dave home, then I wasn't the person I wanted to be.

"Only if you're sure," Maciah said without any judgment in his voice.

He was the most caring and supportive man I'd ever met. Even when he'd ignored me, it was only because of his own guilt and how much I meant to him.

"I'm sure," I said confidently.

"Do you want to go to the bedroom?" he offered, but I declined immediately.

"In no way do I want this to feel sexual." I grimaced, hoping he didn't take offense to that.

He smiled softly. "Then, we'll stay here."

Maciah stood and unbuttoned his suit coat, then

undid the buttons of his dress shirt. Jesus, so much for not making this sexual. My irresistible vampire was going to be half naked, and I'd somehow thought I could keep my hormones in check. *Right*.

My gums were already burning, as if they knew exactly what was coming. My primal instincts were strong, and I wasn't excited about that. My beating pulse intensified as breathing became harder.

Maciah sat on the couch next to me, and I reached for him, needing his closeness.

"Don't think. Just act," he murmured, leaning toward me and kissing my collarbone, which put my mouth dangerously close to the veins protruding from his neck.

I inhaled, searching for the honey smell I'd associated with blood, but only his unique scent coated my tongue. I pressed closer to him, positioning one hand on his thigh while the other buried itself into his dark locks.

He continued to nip along my neck, ear, and collarbone, only staying in one spot for a second or two before further muddling my senses by moving on to the next.

"You are the most stunning creature in this world," he murmured against my heated skin. "Your soul is like the brightest star in the sky calling me home."

My fangs grew as he sweet-talked me, calming my nerves.

"There is nothing in this world you can't overcome, Amersyn. I believe in you."

My grip on his hair tightened, and I forced his head further to the side. I had no choice but to bite him. Not because the action would unlock something powerful inside me, but because my need to have all of him was suddenly something I could no longer control, nor did I want to.

I flicked my tongue out, tasting the saltiness of his skin before leaning closer. Shivers appeared on his skin, turning me on just as much as I knew I was doing to him.

My fangs scraped over his skin, leaving a pink line in their wake without breaking the skin. Maciah groaned beneath me, his fingers digging painfully into my sides as I let the anticipation build between us.

I straddled him, grabbing both of his cheeks, and kissed him as if it might be the last time. My hips rocked forward as my tongue memorized every delectable part of him before running along his jawline and down his neck.

My fangs felt like they were salivating with need as I brushed them over his skin once more. His hand tangled into my hair, urging me closer, and I didn't fight him.

I wanted to hate what I was about to do, but that was the furthest emotion from my thoughts as I opened my mouth and finally bit into my protector.

Where I expected resistance from his tough vampire makeup, there was none. My fangs punctured through his skin smoothly, and blood coated my mouth in the next instance.

Euphoria filled me as I urged my body closer to his. Gulp after eager gulp, I drank him in, and tingles of awareness grew inside me. His feelings were overpowering my every sense. His love for me. His belief in what I could do. His protectiveness over me. All of it had tears burning at the back of my eyes.

Maciah's lips pressed against my neck as I considered pulling back. His hold tightened around me, and the pressure of his own fangs pushed against my skin.

I moaned against him, need continuing to flourish by the second as my body heated from the heightened emotions shared between us. No longer could I remember why I'd been so frightened of biting him.

As I considered pulling back and turning this into something I originally hadn't wanted it to be, Maciah surprised me. Instead of merely nipping at my neck, his fangs cut into me.

My body tensed, but not from fear. I was more

turned on than I'd ever been as he sensually took blood from me.

We were locked together, feeding off one another. Not just with our blood, but with our shared passion and love and so much more.

Vampires weren't supposed to have fated mates, but someone somewhere got that wrong. Magic exploded between the two of us, stitching our souls together and bonding us in a way I never knew existed.

There was no more me. No more Maciah. It was only us. Together as one.

Maciah's hold on me loosened as my fangs began to retract. The moment was ending, but I wasn't ready for the bubble around us to pop. I wanted to live in this moment forever with only my protector.

He trailed his tongue over where his fangs had just been and I did the same before leaning my head against his shoulder, refusing to part from him.

His hands rubbed over my back, brushing my hair out of the way. A hum of satisfaction rumbled through him, making me grin.

"I think that was more than it was supposed to be," I whispered.

"Maybe for normal heirs and protectors, but there is nothing normal about you, Amersyn Holt." Maciah gently pushed me up until he could see my eyes.

"There is nothing, and no one, in this world I will ever love more than you."

I stroked his cheeks. "Nothing will ever tear us apart, no matter what happens."

Our foreheads pressed together, and I closed my eyes, searching inside myself. I might not have been who I once thought I was, or who I thought I wanted to be, but I no longer had any doubts about the changes in my life.

I was exactly where I was supposed to be and surrounded by people that I couldn't imagine my life without any longer.

True acceptance filled my chest and I sighed. "Thank you for believing in me even when I didn't."

His lips brushed across mine. "Always."

CHAPTER 15

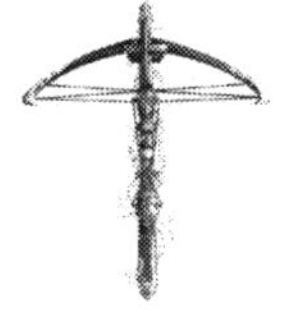

AFTER BONDING WITH MACIAH, I WAS OVERWHELMED with emotions. Not only because of the connection I could feel with Maciah, but the original power as well.

My skin tingled with energy, but I didn't know how to harness whatever was growing inside me. There was something simmering just beneath my skin, yet every attempt at tapping into the power had failed so far.

Maciah's intense stare wasn't helping me focus, either, especially after the heightened emotions we'd shared while biting each other.

"Stop that," I groaned, turning the direction of my pacing to stare at the wall instead of him.

"I'm trying to see if you can hear my thoughts. I guess mind reading is out," he said, not at all disappointed with that fact. I couldn't say I was either.

"Along with mind control, compulsion, emotion control, and anything else we've tried." I tried not to snap at him, but I was growing frustrated, and we were running out of time. Silas had remained silent and, the longer I waited to respond, the more I feared Dave would be punished.

He appeared in front of me, halting my pacing and forcing me to focus only on him. "We'll figure it out. Maybe you need a break."

"We don't have that luxury," I reminded him. Evening was almost upon us, and we had to be ready to face Silas. I wouldn't wait another day to act. As soon as the sun disappeared, I was leaving this house.

I turned back to him, remembering one important thing that I kept forgetting to ask. "How does an original vampire die?"

Maciah grimaced. "Painfully."

"That was already assumed. If Silas wanted to kill me, how would he do that, assuming he knows? We can't guarantee everything will go our way when we face him. I should probably be prepared for the worst-case scenario."

I hated to think that way, but it seemed like the smart choice.

"The past original vampires were staked, chained,

beheaded, and burned to ash with magically made fire," Maciah answered.

"So, one would need a witch to kill me?" I asked.

"Or the right potion, but either way, a witch would need to be involved."

Well, that was a good thing. At least I couldn't be jumped and randomly killed. It would take being captured and a lot of planning. Plenty of opportunity to escape if Silas managed to take me.

Maciah grabbed his phone and typed out a text, but I couldn't see who to. Now that I had my answer, I went back to pacing while trying to figure out what special ability I supposedly had. That could also be something to help keep me alive later on.

Rachel had left the book behind when we'd been given some privacy, but there was nothing else inside that I could find helpful. Biting my protector should have done the trick, according to the ancient vampire who wrote the book.

Then again, I wasn't sure why I would have thought his notes applied to me given that nothing else seemed to.

Rachel, Nikki, and Zeke entered the office with varying expressions on their faces. "What's wrong?" I asked.

All three of them started to respond and I couldn't understand a single word.

I turned to Maciah. "Did you get that?"

He shook his head and nodded toward Zeke. "What happened?"

Zeke blinked several times. "I have no idea."

My face scrunched in confusion. "What do you mean?"

"I, um, never mind. Nothing is wrong. We were just worried about the two of you. You've been in here a long time," he answered, not seeming very sure of his words.

"Did you find a good meeting place for us to suggest to Silas?" Maciah asked.

Nikki pulled out her phone, bringing up a map. "There's an abandoned sawmill north of Salem and in the middle of nowhere. If we can trick him into agreeing on the spot, it's the best place I could find."

My throat began to ache. It had been a few hours since I'd fed and, after the experience with Maciah, I was due for another glass.

Just the thought of blood had my fangs begging to be released, which wasn't something that had happened in a few days. I turned to ask Maciah if he had anything in his office that I could drink, but waves of concern rolling off him had my thoughts changing direction.

"What's wrong?" I asked him.

He nodded toward the others, who were unusually quiet. "Look at them."

Rachel, Nikki, and Zeke were all looking at the

floor, hands fisted at their sides and chests heaving. Zeke's mouth hung open with bared fangs. He slowly looked up at me with crimson eyes. "Stop. Please."

"Stop what?" I had no idea what he was talking about.

Maciah blurred to the small fridge he kept in his office and put a blood bag in my hand. "Drink it."

"Now? Shouldn't we be more worried about them?" I moved to hand the bag to Zeke, but Maciah stopped me.

"You need to drink it. I have more if this doesn't work."

I had no idea what he was talking about, but I trusted him, so I tipped the bag back against my mouth. It was the first time I'd drank from anything other than a cup, but I managed not to make a mess of myself as I emptied half of the bag in one go.

Once I was done, Rachel, Nikki, and Zeke were still tense, but not frozen in place like before.

"What's going on?" I asked, still not understanding.

"You're controlling them. What you're feeling, so are they," Maciah said.

I glanced at the three of them again. The bloodlust was strong. I didn't know how I'd missed it before then. Each of their eyes even had darker red rings around them that I'd never seen before.

Holy crap, I needed to help them. I did my best to change my thoughts from food to a happy moment, except that was almost worse than my hunger. The most recent one was my exchange with Maciah when I'd not only been content but turned on.

Nikki's hands rubbed over her sides, Rachel was biting her lip, and Zeke was adjusting himself. I nearly died of embarrassment.

"How do I make it stop?" I screeched.

"Find where the power is coming from. Focus on what you want and rein it in," Maciah replied, but that seemed easier said than done.

I leaned against his desk and closed my eyes. The new energy inside me was still flowing through my veins, begging to be set free. Every piece of me was charged, and I had no idea where the source of it was.

I took a deep breath and let my shoulders slump, relaxing my body as I did a mental scan of myself. Every bit of power was spread evenly through me, so I started over. I began with my mind, searching for any flicker of something more.

Bright white light swirled within my mind. I envisioned what was flowing through me as soft waves. The energy was strong, but not overwhelming. It wasn't fighting against me or trying to control my actions. As I mentally followed its path, a warmth settled in my chest, calling to me.

Slowly, I moved my attention from my mind to my heart that no longer pumped with my own blood. I searched between the light and shadows inside me, knowing I was close to whatever I needed to find.

There was a flickering of something more—a beating of a pulse that didn't belong to me. I grasped on to that and tensed as a wave of electricity rolled through me. The power didn't attack me, but it also didn't want to be shut down.

Well, that was too damn bad.

I imagined a box of sorts around my heart, one that only I had the key to. I opened the box and directed the energy to flow toward it with promises to be let out later. There was a slight resistance from the power, but I didn't relent in my demands.

The flickering white magic began to retract from my limbs and make its way toward the box I'd hopefully use to control whatever this was. I had no idea if I was going insane, but Maciah had said to rein in the power, and this was the first thing that came to my mind.

As the last bits settled into the trunk, I gently shut the lid. *I promise to let you out again. Just as soon as I figure out what you are.*

And now I was talking to the magical entity inside my body. My day had not at all gone how I had suspected when I got out of bed that morning.

Maciah's palms warmed against my neck.

"Amersyn?" I opened my eyes and he grinned. "There's my girl."

"I need a sex life like yours," Nikki groaned from behind us, and I hid my face against Maciah's chest.

I heard the thud of someone's fist smacking against someone else. "Don't embarrass her or we'll pay the price," Rachel said.

Laughter bubbled inside me, and I double-checked that the energy was still contained. "I have it under control now. I think," I said, peeking around Maciah.

Zeke's eyes were locked on Rachel. Whatever I had made them feel had stuck with the vampire. I couldn't wait until they decided to stop taking things slowly. They were only torturing themselves.

"So, you can control our emotions. Fun," Nikki droned.

Rachel shook her head. "That's not all. I think she can mind-control us as well."

Maciah narrowed his eyes at her. "What do you mean?"

"When we came into the room, she asked a question. I had no control over answering her. My answer was my own, but I didn't willingly give it," Rachel answered, walking toward me. "Mind if I touch you?"

I raised a brow. "Could be fun."

"Get your mind out of the gutter. We've all had

enough of that for the day," she said as her fingers wrapped around my forearm. "Try to send an image to my mind."

"I stuffed the power into a locked box, and I don't think I can let it out that easily," I said.

She squeezed tighter. "Yes, you can. You are the power, Amersyn. It's not separate from you."

Her undying faith in me was a gift I'd never take for granted.

I locked gazes with Rachel and tried to do as she asked of me. As soon as I cracked open the fictional lock on the box, the lid pulsed and began to rise. I slammed it back shut and shook my head. "It's so strong."

"And you're stronger," she replied.

With a deep breath in, I tried again. I could do this. Rachel was right. The power hadn't tried to control me. I didn't need to be afraid of its strength.

On the second attempt, I closed my eyes to focus and coaxed the energy. *Just a little. I don't need all of you. Not yet, but soon. I promise.*

A hum of acceptance rolled through my body as wisps of white magic exited its cage before wrapping around my mind, intertwining with my thoughts.

This could have only been easier if the power talked back and told me how the hell I was supposed to do any of this.

I pictured a beach that my parents used to take us

to during the summers. My toes were in the sand, wind moved the ocean's water with a force to be properly feared, and the sea birds soared above me, searching for their next meal.

"I can taste the salt in the air," Rachel said in awe.

I opened my eyes to find her glancing around the room. "I can see the ocean. Feel the sand under my feet. The office is nowhere to be seen, and neither are you."

"How is that possible?" I asked.

"Projection. You have the ability to trick people into thinking they're somewhere they're not," Maciah said, sounding more worried than ever before.

"How, though? I made them feel my emotions. I forced them all to answer the same question at once. How can I do all three?"

Zeke stepped forward. "You are the last heir alive. Maybe we were wrong. Maybe you weren't meant to only acquire your father's ability. Maybe you were meant to inherit every one of them. From all of your ancestors."

I turned to Maciah. There was still concern flowing through him. "What are you thinking?"

"That we're going to have to worry about more than Silas and Viktor if this gets out to the other nests."

"How did you guys not figure this out once she bit you?" Nikki asked, making a valid point.

"We tried. Nothing I did worked on him," I answered.

"We're bonded. I'm meant to protect you, even if that means I need to do so from yourself, should the power change who you are," Maciah said, and I shuddered at the thought that I could ever need protection from myself.

"How long ago did you figure that out?" I asked.

He grinned. "I assumed after the second time you tried to use your power against me, but I didn't know for sure until the others entered the room."

I returned his smile with a glare. "And you didn't think to share that assumption with me before they came back?"

"If I'd told you, then those thoughts would have been in your head, and you wouldn't have been acting on instinct. Now, you know, and you handled the power in your own way," he said proudly.

Rachel's stare moved between me and Zeke. "I think we need to keep a lot of this as secret as we can. Zeke was able to fight back against the power when he asked Amersyn to stop. We don't know how well this energy of hers would even work against someone like Silas."

"And I could feel it, so it wasn't like I had no idea something was going on that shouldn't have been. I didn't understand it the first time, because it was so brief, but I did the second time," Nikki said.

"So, are you saying this was all for nothing? I can't use these abilities against Silas?" I asked, trying to hide the irritation I could feel building inside me.

"Not at all, but you should be careful when and how you choose to use the magic inside you," Rachel said softly, likely sensing my rising emotions.

Maciah glanced at the clock on his wall. "I think it's time Silas heard from you. Do you think you're ready for that?"

"Absolutely," I answered without hesitation.

I'd spent the last several years keeping people at a distance and reminding myself that I couldn't care too much. I would convince Silas that I was done with Maciah, done being a vampire, and no longer cared what he did, as long as I got what I wanted.

Dave to be free and my vampire existence ended.

CHAPTER 16

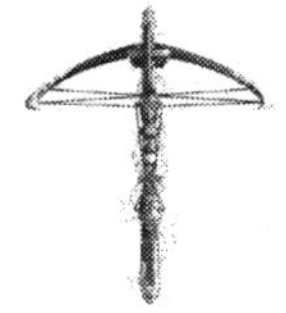

NIKKI HAD THE BRIGHT IDEA THAT I NEEDED TO BE AWAY from the nest before I called Silas. If he was somehow tracking the call and I was still on Maciah's property, it wouldn't matter how convincing my words were. He'd never believe I was telling the truth.

The five of us drove to a nearby park. There was a layer of snow on the ground that hadn't quite melted from the recent storm, but I no longer felt the chill in the air as we walked across the empty playground.

Rachel and Nikki sat on the swings while Zeke stood near them. I didn't care if they heard my conversation, but I didn't want to see them watching me and get distracted, so I turned my back and walked a little further away, leaning against the steps to the jungle gym.

Maciah joined me, but he stood a few feet back. "I'll be right here with you."

"Thank you." I smiled and pulled out my phone, going straight to the message from Silas on Dave's phone. I clicked on his name, then pressed call.

My stomach twisted as nerves ignited inside me and the box around my heart begged to be opened.

Three rings in, I started to worry we'd waited too long. It wasn't until the fifth ring that I heard moaning. "Dave?"

There was a thud followed by a loud groan that was being muffled by something. I tried not to panic and show my concern. I knew I had to keep any feelings locked down or none of our plan was going to work.

I sighed when I wanted to scream. "I don't have time for games, Silas."

"But you had time to wait before calling. I have to admit, I was disappointed you took so long to reach out," he responded.

"Well, I've been busy trying to escape a certain vampire, and I'm not sure what you expected out of me with your message."

He chuckled. "You know, I wasn't sure what to expect, either, which doesn't happen very often. You're quite the contradiction, Ms. Holt."

I smirked. "Thank you."

"I heard you recently went on a little adventure,"

he said, baiting me, and I was going to bite. This was the opening I needed.

"I wouldn't call it an adventure, and it certainly wasn't voluntary," I spat, speaking the truth easily.

"Now, now. Being a vampire isn't so bad. You've had some time to appreciate what our strengths can offer. Don't you want more?"

"More what? Power? Blood?" I scoffed with disgust. "My hate of vampires hasn't changed, Silas. I despise what I've become and the bloodsuckers I've been stuck with."

"Stuck with? You didn't seem to be opposed to them when I saw you before," he said.

I let out a small huff. "Yeah, that was before they failed to do what they promised. I was only using them and now they no longer serve a purpose to me. I've cut my ties with them as of today."

"So, you're looking for a new nest?" Silas sounded intrigued about that. More so than I was comfortable with.

"Not exactly. I do have an offer for you, though. You might think I care that you took Dave, and sure, a part of me does, but that piece of me was tarnished the moment Dmitri killed my human existence."

Silas paused, then spoke without giving away any emotion as to how he felt about my statement. "I'm listening. For now."

Arrogant bloodsucker.

"You know, you're not the only one who hears things. I know you still need my blood. You either didn't get enough before, or something else went wrong. Regardless, I can still give you what you want, but I want something in return." I kept my tone even, but my body was riddled with unease. If I didn't convince Silas I was telling the truth, Dave was dead. The weight of that knowledge was heavier than I liked.

Silas stayed silent as I waited several beats before I let out a soft sigh of boredom. "I don't need you to help, but that small humane part of me left thought this would be a good exchange. Maybe I was wrong. Goodbye, Silas." I pulled the phone away from my ear and held my thumb over the end button.

I had no idea what would happen if I hung up, but I'd laid my cards down anyway and hoped Silas was here to play.

"Wait," he said just as I was convinced that I'd failed.

"For what?" I asked.

"What do you want in return for your blood? I don't assume the bartender is all you want."

I wanted to release the tension in my body as relief filtered through, but the game wasn't over. Not by a long shot.

"You're a smart vampire, Silas. Do I really have to spell this out for you?" I deadpanned.

"You want to die."

I let out a disgusted laugh. "I already did that. Now, I want to end this appalling existence."

"What about this vengeance I've heard you're so hell-bent on?" Silas asked.

"My personal issues are none of your damn business, bloodsucker," I snapped.

He tsked. "I'm very certain it is. If I'm to believe you're truly done with living and not setting me up, then I need all of the answers, Ms. Holt. Even the ones you don't wish to speak of."

I ground my teeth together in real frustration. Silas was triggering me, and I had to let him. I had to show him some vulnerability to make this offer believable.

I lowered my voice and spoke gruffly. "I'd like to think that my family would understand. Four out of five murderers isn't bad, considering the hundreds more I killed along the way. If there's a chance that I get to see them again, regardless of the monster I've been forced to become, then I'll face them proudly."

"You're an interesting woman, Ms. Holt. It's too bad you can't see past your rage. We could have made a powerful team. Even more so than what I speculated you had with Maciah," Silas said, and I knew in that moment I had him right where I wanted.

"I'd never willingly work with vampires. Not

after everything I know now. Maciah and his nest were a means to an end. I'm dead because he couldn't hold up his end of our agreement. I'd have killed him myself if you hadn't presented this opportunity that makes things less complicated for me. I don't want to risk Maciah's nest keeping me alive, and I can't pretend to care for another day. So, you only get one chance to take my offer, Silas. I'm done playing games."

"Okay," was all he said.

"Okay, what?"

"I believe you."

I wanted to reach through the phone and choke Silas. Even though I knew I was the one playing him, he had my emotions worked up as if I believed my words as well.

"Then, give me your address. I'll come to you right now," I said, hoping to work a bit of reverse psychology on him.

He hesitated. "Are you trying to convince me that you didn't figure out where my nest relocated to in Salem?"

I laughed. "Oh, I'm very familiar with where your nest is, but you're a smart vampire, Silas. I don't for one second assume that's where you're staying at the moment. Not when you didn't get what you wanted. That left you open to attack."

I could hear his hum of approval, even through

the phone. "Maciah made a mistake not taking better care of you."

"I'm not on the phone to chat about that prick. If you won't tell me where you are, then let's meet somewhere neutral," I said, slightly wincing at my harsh words.

"Anywhere you have in mind?" he asked, but I wasn't stupid. He was testing me. I still hadn't completely convinced him of my wants.

"I have several, but I doubt you trust me enough that you'd let me pick, so let's quit with the games, Silas. Where are we meeting? My patience is running out."

"Such a waste." He sighed.

Yeah, I knew I was a prize, but that bastard wouldn't ever get the chance to put me on his shelf.

"There are dark alleys, shut-down sawmills, deserted farmhouses. All of them somewhere between wherever you are and I am. Take your pick, vampire. Just do so now," I snapped.

"That's the problem with new vampires. They lack the patience to truly enjoy this lifestyle, but fortunately for you, I'm eager to finish this as well. What farmhouse?" he asked, and my heart sank that he didn't take the right bait.

"The one I killed a nest in last year is just ten miles outside of Salem," I said, hoping that it was too close to his nest to be appealing.

"And the sawmill?"

Mother-effing bingo.

"A few miles outside of Aurora. Halfway between Portland and Salem," I said.

"As appealing as a dark alley sounds, I'd rather not be interrupted. I'll see you at the sawmill no sooner than ten tonight. If you're there early and I suspect a setup, then you'll never see me or your bartender again."

Silas hung up, and I took a deep breath, finally searching for Maciah. He wasn't next to me any longer, but I could sense him near me, along with a whole lot of rage building inside him.

He was standing between the braces of the swing set, fists squeezed so tightly they were bending the metal frame. I was standing in front of him within the next second. "I'm sorry."

"You did what you had to. My guilt is not your problem." His voice was rough and full of fury.

"I didn't mean what I said. You know that, right?"

His dark eyes landed on me, sending chills down my spine. "Maybe not all of it, but there were truths in there, Amersyn. Don't lie to me and say there weren't."

"You're right. I'd rather be human. I'd rather not be this vampire heir that people want dead. But I don't hate what I've become either. Not anymore. And that's because of you. I'm exactly where I want to be, given the circumstances. Right here. With you. That, you can believe."

Maciah was hurting, and it was my fault. He was blaming himself and I didn't know how to make him think otherwise.

"I do believe you, but that doesn't mean I don't hold myself accountable for the things that have happened to you."

I grabbed on to the lapels of his suit, forcing him toward me. "Don't let those bastards win. If you pull away from me out of guilt again, then they get the last laugh. I won't lie to you and pretend all of this was okay with me, but I know that regardless of how I felt, I'm exactly where I'm supposed to be."

His hands released the metal frame and found my face as his lips met my mouth. He held me tightly, kissing me with every bit of agony I knew he was holding on to. "I'm sorry," he murmured.

"Just don't let them win."

"Never."

I turned around to find Rachel, Nikki, and Zeke were nowhere to be seen.

"They went back to the car as soon as the call ended," Maciah said.

"Smart vampires," I said.

He glowered. "They've learned my moods over the years."

"I'm surprised they've put up with you for so long," I teased.

Maciah picked me up, tossed me over his shoulder, and smacked my ass so hard that the sound echoed through the empty playground. "When this is all over, I'm going to own that smart mouth of yours."

"I eagerly await the execution of that threat."

CHAPTER 17

As soon as we got back to the mansion, Maciah and Zeke went to prepare the vampires that would be coming with us. It didn't matter that Silas had made it clear I couldn't arrive before ten. We'd still have vampires near enough to act as soon as it was necessary.

I went to my room and stared at my closet. I had no idea what one was supposed to wear on their way to die, but also be prepared to fight in. I decided to go with my normal hunter gear, because Silas would expect me to be leery of him even if I wanted to end my vampire existence.

Black leather pants I hadn't worn in a while seemed dramatic yet fitting. Those went on first along with my boots that could store stakes for me. I peeked for a shirt, but nothing seemed right for my mood.

Nikki and Rachel entered my closet to find me standing in only my pants and bra. "Trouble dressing for your date?" Nikki joked.

"Girl problems." I shrugged.

"I vote for all black. You can't ever go wrong with that," Rachel said.

She wasn't wrong. I grabbed a tank top and slid the smooth material over my head. Before I left my closet, I searched for my crossbow.

"Hello, old friend," I cooed as my hands wrapped around the carbon fiber stock.

"You don't really need that anymore," Nikki said.

"Just because you don't need something doesn't mean it isn't good to have," I replied with a wink.

I put the strap of the bow over my shoulder and sighed as it fit snugly across my chest. Yes, this felt right. My hunter adrenaline was already kicking in and we weren't leaving for another hour. I was going to need more blood to keep myself in check.

"You're not going to stop, are you?" Rachel asked, nodding to my crossbow.

"Stop killing vampires? Absolutely not. If you guys really want to bring back the old ways, then someone needs to keep the population of the bad bloodsuckers down. I'm happy to do that." Rachel and Nikki might not understand the thrill I got, but that was okay. I wouldn't be the same hunter I was before, but I knew I'd never stop.

Our world couldn't afford for me to.

"How did you get into this?" Rachel asked hesitantly, knowing I didn't like to talk about my past.

My eyes found Nikki's, thankful she'd kept my story to herself so I could tell Rachel myself.

Walking out of the closet, I pulled my crossbow off, setting it next to me as I sat on the couch in my room while Rachel and Nikki took the bed. This time, there was no hesitation or pain as the words spewed from my mouth, telling Rachel about Caleb and the way we'd ended things.

"How did you get away from him?" Rachel asked.

"I had more money than I knew what to do with by then. When my own threats didn't work on Caleb, I used the other hunters. I was like a little sister to most of our crew. When Caleb was ousted from the group, he disappeared. I have no idea where he went or what he's doing now, but I don't care. He emotionally abused me for too long. I was just lucky I had the means to get free."

"And the will. You were strong enough to know when something wasn't right and get out before things escalated. Not all who end up in a similar position understand that emotional abuse is still abuse and it's okay to leave," Nikki added, speaking the absolute truth.

Our world was a screwed-up place.

"Thank you for sharing. I know you don't like to do that often," Rachel said.

"What's a womance between three girls without divulging the shadows of our past?" I knew the only way to move on from them was to stop letting them hold power over me.

"What are you going to do when you face Silas?" Nikki asked.

I shrugged. "No idea. I'm better at winging things, but I do know my priority will be getting Dave out. Whoever gets him when he walks out of the mill has to take him far away from the fight."

"What if Silas won't let him go first?" Rachel asked, and I'd already thought of that.

"I have these new abilities. I'll have to put them to real use at some point. Maciah doesn't want me to show my hand too early, and I won't, but I'm also not afraid to unleash them and see what happens if that's what is needed," I answered.

"You should practice on us while we wait," Nikki suggested.

I'd already done that once and I wasn't really thrilled about messing with their minds, but trying a few new things that I'd been curious about wasn't a bad idea.

"You'll need to get me some blood," I said to Nikki, looking only at her while letting a bit of my power bleed out.

She was off the bed in one second and at the door in the next. I laughed as she blurred into the hallway. Maybe this would be more fun than I thought.

Rachel grinned at me. "You're evil."

"And yet you still love me."

"Truth, girl. Now, try something on me, but don't make me leave the room," she said, crossing her legs and sitting up against the headboard.

I had no idea what I wanted to do to Rachel. As a few things came to mind, I focused more on the power I harnessed inside me. I knew the box I was keeping the energy contained in was only a bandage. I could already feel the pulsing of the magic wanting to be free, but I wasn't ready for that.

Closing my eyes, I cracked open the lid again, coaxing the eager power out, urging the flow of white wisps to move along my veins and out to my arms.

I flexed my fingers, extending the ability all the way to the tips as I turned my palm up. I envisioned the magic traveling from me to Rachel, aiming right for her heart as I watched her face.

Her eyes widened and darkened as her hands gripped her knees. She sucked in a breath, then exhaled loudly. "I can feel you," she whispered.

"What do you feel?" I asked.

"Grief, anger, determination, a fearlessness like I've never known. How are you doing this?" she asked in awe.

I wasn't sure how to answer her. I hadn't even known what I was going to do until it was already happening. Rachel had been honest with me from day one. She'd been the person to believe I could see past my hatred long enough to hear her out. I wanted to give her this gift of insight to the darkness I held inside myself, so she could better understand how she changed me.

She had tears brimming in her eyes. "Thank you."

I nodded, not wanting to make a big deal out of it.

"I could sense your power, though. I knew what I was feeling wasn't me. If you have any hope of tricking someone like Silas or Viktor, you'll need to find a way to tone down your energy. It's too strong to be subtle," she said, thankfully moving the conversation along.

You hear that, vamp magic? We need stealth, not a grand entrance.

My chest warmed, and I wasn't sure if that was a good thing or not. I'd never been one to talk to myself before, but ever since this power appeared, it seemed natural. Almost as if the energy was a separate entity inside me, even though Rachel was convinced it wasn't.

Nikki came back into the room with a tray of cups and blood bags. She held the platter with one hand and pointed at me with a sneer. "Not cool."

I laughed. "I'd say I'm sorry, but you'd know that was a lie."

She sat the blood on the bed, and I was up, ready for my next serving. They'd mentioned we'd need to feed more than usual before a fight, and I took that seriously, especially if I had any plans of using the power inside me. Something told me that once I truly unleashed its strength on someone that I didn't care about, I'd have to be careful not to drain myself in the process.

The sweet nectar of honey-tasting crimson coated my mouth as I took my first drink. I never imagined that I could be okay with this part of being a vampire, but maybe it was knowing that the blood was donated and not stolen from unwilling, innocent humans that made things easier.

There was also no denying my natural cravings. I hadn't been near humans since that first day, but I hoped with bagged blood, I wouldn't have to worry about losing control if I went into a public setting.

When I finished my cup, I set it back down on the tray and placed my hand on Nikki's shoulder. "Thank you." As I did that, I attempted to control her thoughts on a small scale, picturing the warmth of the sunshine I missed so much shining down on us.

Nikki squinted and glanced around the room before shaking her head. "I think there was something wrong with that blood." Then, she rubbed both hands over her arms.

"Are you okay?" Rachel asked.

"My eyes feel super sensitive to the light like it's brighter than it should be, and I feel hot. I don't know. This hasn't ever happened to me," Nikki answered.

My hand was still on her shoulder, and I gave it a squeeze, shutting down the energy. "You really couldn't feel me?" I asked.

She gaped. "That was you? No, I honestly thought there was something wrong with me and I was going to be pissed if I couldn't go with you guys. I feel fine now."

"What did you do?" Rachel asked.

"I pictured the warmth of the sun. Probably not the best idea now that I think about it, but it was the first thing that came to mind." I had no idea how Nikki did in the sun. Even though the magic was only an illusion of the mind, she could have freaked out.

"That was impressive. Can you do that without touching me?" she asked.

"I can try." When I was holding Nikki's shoulder, I had more control over the power, but I had a feeling commanding the energy by touch wasn't going to be the way I learned to master its abilities.

WE CONTINUED TO WORK ON VARIOUS USES OF MY NEW talents, but touch was still the best way for me to remain undetected while using the power. I had a feeling that wouldn't be a problem with Silas. He didn't seem like the kind of bloodsucker who was afraid to get up close and personal.

After we all drank one more serving of blood, we left my room in search of Maciah and Zeke. They weren't in Maciah's office, so Nikki suggested that we check out back. Sure enough, both of them and Eddie were standing in front of a group of about twenty-five vampires.

That was the first time I'd seen so many of Maciah's nest gathered together. Normally, they kept to smaller groups of five-to-seven. Seeing all of their muddy-red eyes and determined faces dressed in tactical drab I was used to seeing around here made me feel better about heading out.

I knew I was capable of killing Silas, but that was in a fair fight. Everything I'd learned about the power-hungry bloodsucker told me that there would be nothing fair about this meet-up, but I tried not to let that knowledge overcast my thoughts. If Silas wanted to play dirty, then so could I.

"We're going to take every vehicle we have, but only drive them as far as ten miles from the mill. Amersyn will be going in first by herself, and she will have comms on her that are linked only to me. I will give the final signal when everyone is to move in. You're not to act for any reason before that," Maciah said to the vampires before him.

"If any of Silas's men cross your path before we make ourselves known, your job is to kill them silently and search them for comms of their own. If we can hear their plans, that would be best," Zeke added.

"You all know what tonight means to us. Silas has impacted each of us in some way or another, even if you never had to live with him. We can't let him get away this time. No matter what," Maciah said as I approached his side.

I grabbed his hand, giving him a quick nod as he continued. "Amersyn will be offering herself up to him in exchange for a human named Dave. We have no idea what kind of condition Dave is in. Whoever finds him first needs to pick him up and take him back to the vehicles and let me know as soon as that's done."

Eddie stepped up next to provide further instructions about how the vampires would be split up into groups and where they were to wait for the green light.

I listened intently as Eddie spoke, so that I'd know where the friendly vamps were supposed to be when the chaos started.

Maciah pulled me away from where we stood. Zeke, Rachel, and Nikki followed until we were back at the driveway. There was a small black SUV waiting for us.

"I assume this is our ride?" I asked.

Zeke nodded, jumping into the driver's seat. "We have ten of these. Every group will be driving in the same thing, but we're all leaving at different times. Eddie is giving the schedule out now. We're up first."

Rachel and Nikki opened the back door, getting in next. I moved to join them, but Maciah tugged me back. "If at any point you're unsure if Silas is still buying the plan that you've laid out, you need to say something. I won't lose you, even if that means the bastard gets to live another day."

"I have no intentions of dying tonight," I said, pushing up onto my toes and giving him a kiss. "We have a good plan. We know Silas will, too. The rest will fall into place however it's going to. If we let worry in, then we'll second-guess our choices, and that's when we lose."

His hands tightened around my waist as I pressed

my head against his chest. "I don't like it when you make a good point that puts your life at risk."

"Life isn't worth living if we let fear dictate our choices," I murmured against him.

"Then, let's make it worth living forever."

CHAPTER 18

AN HOUR LATER, WE ARRIVED AT OUR DESIGNATED SPOT. Three other SUVs were supposed to meet us there, and the rest would be divided up at two other locations. The sky was dark, thanks to the new moon. There were no lights around us and only a slight wind blowing in our direction.

I double-checked that my crossbow was loaded and slid it back into place, rubbing my thumb absentmindedly along the leather strap holding the weapon to my chest.

"Fifteen minutes until the meet time," Nikki announced, dressed identical to Rachel in form-fitting charcoal cargo pants and a black tee. They each had small daggers strapped to their thighs and peeking out from their boots, along with clear earpieces they pulled from their front pockets.

"Am I getting one of those? Also, rude I wasn't included in the matching wardrobe," I said, mostly joking. I just hadn't noticed back at the house that I was the odd woman out.

Maciah approached me, clipping a silver hoop to the top of my ear. "No. You're not supposed to be part of our team, so you don't get to match."

Yeah, I probably should have thought of that on my own.

"This hoop will only allow me to hear you. Once the ruse is up, you'll want to put this in." He handed me the same earpiece the rest of them had. "Then, you'll be able to hear the rest of us and communicate if needed."

"I'm assuming you don't want me to hear you while I'm with Silas because that means he'd be able to pick up on your voice as well?" I asked as I tugged on the clipped earring to confirm it was secure.

"Correct. As much as I don't like you facing him alone, you've set up a good plan. We can't put that at risk for the convenience of communication. I'll be close enough that I can be at your side in a matter of seconds, though. You won't be alone." He gave my hand a reassuring squeeze, but it wasn't necessary.

I already knew I could trust these vampires to have my back. Funny how I never trusted the hunters that way. I wondered if that was merely because of my past with Caleb or because I'd always known I was different from them. I just hadn't known *how* different until I met Maciah.

"It's time for you to go," Rachel said, worry showing between her creased brows.

I nodded, slipping the earpiece into my front pocket and pulling away from Maciah. I didn't want some dramatic parting. That meant we believed there was a chance we wouldn't see each other again. I wouldn't let those negative thoughts inside my head.

Maciah seemed to understand what I needed, because he didn't pull me back to him this time. "I'll see you soon," I said to him.

"Yes, you will."

Nikki wrapped an arm around Rachel, keeping her back as I turned away from the family I thought I'd never have again. Knowing I had them to fight for was enough to keep my steps even as I left them behind.

Shadows from the trees swallowed me up, and I didn't stop until I was sure the others could no longer see me. I rested a hand against one of the oak trees and took a deep breath. I could do this. I needed to remember my hatred of vampires like Silas and apply that to myself. I wanted my disgust for this new life to be so strong that Silas would be able to taste it as soon as he saw me.

I pictured Viktor squeezing the life out of my mother before tearing her throat out. My brother's broken body on the floor. My father's body torn apart throughout the living room.

Lastly, the laughter of the vampires as they sped away, believing they'd succeeded with their task.

My nails dug into the bark of the tree, cutting through the wood as my rage built. Blood. Death. Vengeance. That was all that mattered. Once I had that mindset, only then was I ready to face Silas.

I sped forward at full speed, only stopping at the edge of the property line of the mill to check the time. There was one minute left.

I fisted my hands at my side as my narrowed eyes searched the abandoned building for vampires ready to end my existence.

Forms moved through the darkness, but too fast for me to identify anyone. Silas had brought a team with him, as expected. I inhaled, searching for scents, and focused my hearing.

Twenty-eight vampires crossed my senses, which meant our fight would at least be even, but I couldn't focus on that as the sound of a heart struggling to beat and labored breathing caught my attention.

Dave.

He was hurt. Badly.

Time was up. I stepped onto the cracked pavement with weeds growing along the dark surface. There was a door open, and I blurred right through it, stopping only for a moment to search for Dave's weakened heartbeat.

I followed that, ignoring the taste of his sweet blood that filled the air as I got closer to him. I went around three corners and up two sets of stairs before I found them.

My bartender was crumpled on the ground in the fetal position. Silas was standing next to him, looking older than the last time I'd encountered the vampire leader.

His previously dark-blond hair had streaks of grey, highlighted by the swinging overhead light. The creases around his eyes were deep and extended into his temples. Even the wrinkles around his mouth and forehead were more defined. I'd never seen anything like it on a vampire, no matter how old they were.

Whatever Silas had done while trying to take on my powers had further wounded him, but only time would tell if it had weakened him as well.

"It's lovely to see you again, Ms. Holt," he said with a fake grin.

"Cut the crap, Silas. We're not friends. We're a means to an end for each other, but it doesn't appear you're keeping up with your part of the deal." I nodded to Dave. "I wanted him alive."

"He is. Doesn't the blood still pumping through him call to you?"

I bared my fangs, playing along. "It disgusts me."

Silas shook his head at me. "Such a waste, but I am a vampire of my word. Dave is breathing, and I will take your life just as soon as I get what I want."

Warning bells went off for me. Silas didn't intend to kill me in this mill. I wasn't specific enough in my demands.

"How am I supposed to know that Dave will live after I'm dead if he can't walk out of here?" I asked, trying to stall whatever Silas had planned.

"True leaders don't lie. I have no reason to break our deal. You care about saving humans from vampires. If that's your last wish, I will honor it." He glared at me as if my lack of faith in the psycho appalled him.

"Yeah, that doesn't work for me. My hate for vampires runs deep enough that I'm willing to end my life just to stop being this monster. I don't care what you say about your 'honor', Dave needs to walk away from here, or the deal is off. I'll find a hunter to help me instead," I said, hoping my threat was enough to make him show a bit of his plans.

He chuckled and shook his head. "You have no idea what you are, do you? A hunter can't kill you."

I did my best to hide my surprise from his words. Did he know something that Maciah didn't? From the answer he'd given about how an original died, there didn't seem to be any reason why a hunter couldn't kill me.

Sure, it would be damn near impossible if I wasn't willing, but I was pretending to be, so that didn't make sense. Unless Silas assumed no witch would dare do business with a hunter. That could make sense. Either way, I wasn't going to back down from my bluff of considering other options.

"I know exactly who I am and how I will die. With a little assistance, there isn't anything a hunter can't do," I replied with crossed arms.

Silas cocked his head to the side, gauging my words. "Lies," he spat.

Four vampires flanked each of his sides before I could take my next breath. They hissed, glaring at me with beady red eyes.

My hands went to my crossbow, pulling it over my head and aiming the already loaded stake at Silas. "If a single one of you moves any closer to me, your leader is dead," I threatened.

"There's the hunter I've heard so much about. Now, tell me, Ms. Holt. How many of Maciah's vampires did you bring with you?"

"What are you talking about?" I asked, hoping he was bluffing himself.

He waggled a finger at me. "Again, you surprise me. This time with your stupidity. There isn't a trick you can pull that I haven't already done myself. My men are already circling the property. I'm just curious if I'll be able to end Maciah's entire nest in one night, or if there will be leftovers to clean up."

Damn it. He knew. He'd played me this whole time, and I'd fallen for it, even though I'd known there would be a trap.

I didn't bother to reply to him. There was no point. Instead, I pulled the trigger on my crossbow, nailing the vampire nearest to Silas dead center in his heart. "Give me Dave and we can walk away from this."

I knew if I killed Silas first, then everything would turn to chaos. If I could get Dave out of the way, then there would be no holding back.

"You're in no position to demand anything. You only have so many stakes. What will you do when you run out?" he asked, voice full of curiosity as the vampire I shot turned into a cloud of shimmering ash. Though, my odds of winning didn't increase. More vampires crept out of the shadows behind Silas.

"Whatever I have to," I spat, hoping Maciah and the rest of them were already moving in. I couldn't chance putting my earpiece in to find out and getting distracted for even the briefest of seconds.

He nodded toward the vampires remaining at his sides, and they sped ahead, fangs bared for me and hissing like banshees.

"Now, Maciah," I demanded as I quickly fired off two more stakes through my crossbow before grabbing the last one and tossing the weapon out of the way.

Two of the remaining seven vampires disappeared mid-run, but the other five leapt for me all at once. I staked a fourth, hoping to hold on to my weapon, repeating the process as many times as I needed, but as the metal tip of the stake struck its target, one of the other vampires barreled into my side, sending me ten feet in the other direction and forcing me to let go of the stake.

I landed with an echoing thud against a steel beam holding the ceiling to this floor up and smacking the back of my head. Only a short burst of pain rocked through me, then I was back on my feet, pulling two stakes from my boots.

Vampires appeared behind me, grabbing both of my arms and trying to jerk me backward. I fought against their hold and rolled forward, bending my wrists at painful angles until my arms slipped free from their hold and I somersaulted just out of reach.

Except there were more bloodsuckers in front of me. Mother effer. They were like cockroaches crawling out of the shadows.

I could hear commotion downstairs, but that didn't fill me with hope. We were a long way from winning this fight. I pushed off my feet, gaining air from my speed and force. I aimed my boots toward the nearest vampire's chest and sent him tumbling into the two others behind him.

Back on my feet, I jumped into the pile of vampires I'd just made and stabbed the first chest I could see. He snapped the stake in half, but it was too late. As soon as he began to shrivel up, I moved on to the next one.

Just as I raised my arm, someone yanked on my hair and lifted me up into the air before grabbing my neck with his other hand, turning me toward him.

I still had another stake in my hand. I moved to stab the vamp in the heart, but I froze as the familiar face registered with me.

"Caleb?"

"Hello, Syn."

CHAPTER 19

No, this couldn't be real. Caleb couldn't be a vampire. He was one of the best hunters I'd ever known. He would have rather died than be turned. It was something he always pounded into me during training.

Yet, his red eyes were undeniable.

Caleb's grip tightened around my neck as he took the stake from my hand and brought me closer to his face. "No warm welcome for the man that made you into who you are?"

"Screw you," I spat in his face, finally breaking through my initial shock.

Caleb chuckled darkly. "Oh, Syn. I've tested those goods. There's no reason to do so again."

He was purposely trying to rile me with the insult

and by using the nickname he'd given me the day we met. He used to tell me that it would help me move on from my past, separating the daughter I no longer was to the hunter I needed to be.

Except I wasn't the same person he met all those years before. Hell, I wasn't even the same as I was two months ago.

It was time to show these bloodsuckers who Amersyn Holt was born to be.

For the first time since arriving at the abandoned mill, I unlocked the box containing my original power. The energy flowed through my veins, warming my insides as it moved through my extremities, doing exactly as I commanded.

Caleb flashed his fangs at me. "What? Not in the mood for catching up? That's disappointing."

Yeah, he wasn't going to get anything else out of me. I refused to give him that power. Not anymore.

I pushed my energy out, willing it to convince Caleb that his skin was burning to ash from the inside out. As I glared at him, his jaw tensed, and he squeezed tighter around my neck.

"Something wrong?" I wheezed.

He glanced down at his chest as if searching for a stake in his heart. "I…"

I smirked at him as his arm holding me lowered enough that I could touch the floor again. I kicked off the hard surface and brought one of my knees up when Caleb's body started to tremble. My initial hit caught Caleb right in his junk. He sucked in a breath from the unexpected impact, and his hold on me loosened just enough that I could get free.

Knowing my energy was keeping him incapacitated, I focused on the threats still close by. The other vampires I'd been fighting made a move for me again, but I was ready for that. Swirling around, I pulled another stake from my boot and stabbed the nearest bloodsucker as Caleb began to convulse on the ground behind me. Served that traitorous prick right.

Once the shock of seeing him again had worn off, the adrenaline of the fight soared through me and reignited my drive to kill Silas. I slashed through the vampires, releasing more and more of the power inside me, using it to debilitate the vampires I couldn't kill in my efforts to keep them from capturing me.

There were four vampires thrashing on the ground from the temporary nightmare I'd locked them in and only three more left standing that I intended to turn into ash.

They blurred toward me at once, but I was ready. I swung my arm back, waiting for one of them to grab on to me before bringing my stake forward.

Except that never happened.

The vampires went wide, moving past me. Before I could turn around, multiple sets of hands latched onto my arms, jerking me back while simultaneously pushing me to the ground. My face slammed into the concrete floor, my cheek taking the brunt of the impact since my arms were wrenched behind me.

The jolt stunned me, and I lost hold of the power inside me. The magic retreated back inside its box, the hinges of the lid vibrating just as fiercely as my head was.

Two seconds of being stunned was all the vampires needed to haul me back up and restrain my hands with some sort of chain that I couldn't break through, but also wasn't burning my skin. I shook the hair out of my face and Silas was in front of me.

"What did you do to my vampires?" he asked me, voice full of curiosity, not anger.

My lips thinned. I wasn't telling that bastard a damn thing.

He backhanded me, getting so close to my face that our noses almost touched when I looked back up. "I played your game long enough, Ms. Holt. It's time for you to play mine. Your friends are all dead, and you're going to be next if you don't cooperate."

I didn't believe him for one second. The others couldn't be dead. They'd never leave me alone like I'd been for so long.

Maciah was smarter than other vampires. Zeke

was stronger than them. Rachel was faster. Nikki was more conniving. They had each earned my trust, as well as my faith in their talents.

I tugged at the restraints on my hands, but they were ironclad. Two of the vampires were still holding on to me, and I decided to screw with Silas a little more. The bastard didn't scare me. If he was going to kill me, he'd have done so by then. He needed me alive, and I was going to make him wish he didn't.

My power crept out of its cage as I held Silas's crimson gaze. He wasn't touching me, but I wasn't trying to hide what I was capable of any longer.

Silas's eyes darted past my head, but I didn't let whatever distracted him stop my momentum. The white energy trickled out of me, only my eyes seeing its movements. I commanded the energy to wrap around Silas like a cocoon, then make him feel powerful and on top of the world.

He glanced back at me, smirking. "There is no way out of this for you. I will get what I want."

"No, you won't." As the words left my mouth, I was pulled back to the ground. Daggers went flying over my head, narrowly missing Silas.

Damn it, I'd been so close. My hold on the power inside me broke once again, but I wasn't done. The vampires holding me had been hit with the daggers, and I was yanked back up to my feet.

"Miss me?" Rachel's smiling face appeared in my peripherals as she worked at the chain around my wrists.

"Just a bit. Everyone else okay?" I asked. Even though I was convinced they weren't dead like Silas had said, that didn't mean they were in good shape.

Whatever Rachel was using to free my hands burned my skin and she winced. "Sorry. And yes, we're hanging in there."

While Rachel continued working to get me free, I searched for Silas. He wasn't on the ground any longer, and neither was Caleb. When I'd lost my concentration the last time, any sort of mind control I'd had over the other vampires must have disappeared.

"Got it," Rachel said another second later, but I couldn't care about being free from the chains any longer.

The room was too quiet. Everyone was gone, aside from the two of us and a likely dying Dave.

I went to him, kneeling down and pressing my hand gently against his bruised cheeks. His auburn hair was matted with blood and all I wanted was to see his light blue eyes. "I can hear your heart, but you have to give me something more, Dave."

I was afraid to move him, but I couldn't leave him there, either. Rachel joined me and helped me lift him as carefully as possible. There was a small office in the corner, and we carried him there, laying him down on his side in case he started coughing up blood.

Rachel checked him over as best she could with the mere seconds we had. "He's not waking up and his heartbeat is low, but steady. We can't do anything for him here unless you want to turn him."

I sneered at her. "Absolutely not." My gaze moved back to Dave. "If you can hear me, you better keep fighting to stay alive. I'll be back just as soon as these bastards are dead."

I stood and left the room without looking back. I had to keep moving forward for Dave and the others. There was nothing any of us could do until we killed these bloodsuckers.

Rachel was at my side, arms out and ready to fight. "Do you have a plan?"

I closed my eyes, listening for sounds of vampires. There were still plenty of battles happening on the lower levels, but that wasn't where Silas would be.

"Up," I said, then grabbed two of my stakes that had been left on the ground before blurring out of the room toward the stairs.

Rachel was right on my ass as we ran. I considered searching out Maciah first, but I didn't want to give Silas the chance to get away—not again. We'd already used up too much time moving Dave, but my conscience wouldn't let me leave him there for anyone to stumble upon. At least out of the way, he had a chance to survive.

We passed two more levels with locks on the doors before we found the roof access. The door was closed, but there was no lock.

I glanced back at Rachel. "I don't know what we're walking into up here. You don't have to join me, because this could very well be a death sentence, but I can't walk away."

"Ride or die. That's how our womance works." Her hand pressed to the earpiece I'd forgotten all about.

I reached for mine while she was listening to whatever was happening on the other end, but my fingers only pulled out broken pieces of plastic from my pocket.

"What's happening?" I asked Rachel.

"They're trying to make their way to us, but things aren't going as smoothly as Maciah hoped."

As much as I wanted to ask what she meant by that and possibly go back for them, we didn't have that luxury. Not unless it was life or death.

"Do they need our help? If not, we have to go," I said, hand reaching for the handle.

Rachel shook her head, tightening the ponytail at the base of her neck at the same time. "Let's go."

"Ride or die," I murmured as I cracked the door open, hoping like hell I wasn't about to get my best friend killed.

Wind whistled around us, blowing in strong from the east, and I paused, trying to get a handle on the scents swirling around us. Everything was muddled from the weather, and I couldn't tell how many vampires might be around or who they might be.

I assumed Caleb had fled with Silas. The thought of killing the man who taught me about vampires and led me down the road of my purpose hadn't crossed my mind before. Not even when he'd been so controlling in the end.

It was hard to see him as only a bloodsucker that needed to die, but I was going to have to separate who Caleb once was from what he was now. He was no longer a man, or even a hunter. He was a vampire. One who was working alongside a power-hungry psycho.

I wasn't afraid to do whatever was necessary, but killing Caleb wasn't likely to be preemptive.

Rachel's hand rested between my shoulder blades as we crept onto the rooftop. Everything was dark, but my enhanced eyes didn't need light to see what I was looking for.

Silas stood at the edge of the rooftop with several

vampires on each side of them—none of which were Caleb.

Rachel moved to my side as we approached and I directed my power, urging the energy to hug my skin, simmering just beneath the surface.

"Get her," Silas demanded as our paces slowed.

I still had the two stakes I'd grabbed from the other room, but slipped them into my back pockets, opting for brute force instead. If Silas wanted to see the monster I'd become, then he was going to get a front row seat to the show.

Two sets of hands landed on me. I considered using mind control to make this easier, but I was more than this power. I didn't need to depend on it for my strength.

One of them wrapped their arms around my waist while the other went for my arms, but I was faster than both of them. I let the first keep hold of me as I focused on the second. My hand wrapped around his neck, and I bared my fangs at him as I considered ripping his head right off.

His nails scored my biceps, trying to keep me still, but these vampires were nothing compared to the original power coursing through my body.

Just before I made my next move, Rachel stumbled next to me, but she recovered quickly and staked the vampire that had been trying to kill her.

She grinned at me before swirling around to backhand another incoming attacker.

I refocused on the vampires trying to restrain me without killing me. There were chunks of my shirt missing and rips in my pants, but none of their attempts at hurting me had even made me flinch. I was either a hell of a lot stronger than I'd realized or Silas had some of the weakest vampires around fighting for him.

I reached out and dug my fingers into the vampire's neck that was nearest. He continued to claw at my arms, but any damage he made healed before pain could even register with me.

My nails cut into his flesh as I tightened my grip. The vampire at my waist sank his fangs into my ribs, actually hurting me for the first time. I loosened my hold on the other, but before he could get away, Rachel swooped in and yanked the biter off me.

With no other distractions, I relieved the first vampire of his head with my bare hands and went with a bit of dramatics as I flung the head toward Silas's feet before it turned to ash.

I didn't bother to wait for his response before moving to defend myself from another relentless attack. I ducked and twisted, staying just out of reach from the new vampire. He blurred and must have jumped over me, because my arms were suddenly pinned behind my back. It was unfortunate for these vampires that they couldn't kill me. It only meant they were sure to die.

I hit the vampire with a bit of my energy, forcing him to release me as I reached around for one of the stakes I tucked away after first arriving on the rooftop.

As he stood there, eyes glazed over and confused, I leaned in closer and pulled my energy back. "You should have never chosen to fight for someone else when they'd never fight for you in return," I said, then plunged the stake into his chest.

There was a moment of clarity in the vampire's blood-red eyes as he realized the mistake that he'd made in fighting for Silas. *Too late, bloodsucker.*

I glanced around to find Rachel, seeing that she'd taken down her fair share of opponents and it was only Silas standing before us. She couldn't kill him since he'd created her, but I had no ties to the power-hungry vampire. My blood hadn't done anything for him.

My skin pulsated with energy that swirled inside me and provided me with the confidence I needed to end this nightmare.

I tightened my hands into fists, calling on whatever powers I'd inherited from the original vampires, grateful for them and wishing the world hadn't been drawn to the evil that had ended their way of existence.

For the first time since becoming a vampire, I felt acceptance from deep within me of my true form. I was a vampire. My human existence had only been a small part of me, but as I stood before Silas, ready to end his life, I knew this was the path I was always meant to take.

I expected him to try to talk me down, to bribe me with the things he thought held value in this life. Instead, Silas stood there smirking as if he didn't have a care in the world.

My steps drew me closer to him as I urged my power forward, wanting to take over his mind, bring the bastard to his knees, and rid him of his head.

As my energy made contact with him, he shook a finger at me. "I wouldn't do that if I was you, Ms. Holt."

"Why the hell not?" I retorted, pressing in on him.

A muffled moan sounded from behind me. I didn't want to take my eyes off Silas, but I couldn't sense Rachel next to me anymore.

My stomach sank as I quickly checked where the noise had come from. Rachel was on her knees. Caleb had one hand over her mouth, and another was holding one of my stakes over her chest, the tip already buried just under her skin.

"You came here to exchange your life for another's. How about we make that happen now?" Silas said, voice full of confidence.

Mother-effing bastard.

I cast another glance at Rachel. She shook her head at me. She was ready to die if it meant Silas did too, but I couldn't let that happen. I couldn't make that choice even if she supported it.

I regrettably pulled my power back inside me, and Silas grinned. "Good girl."

CHAPTER 20

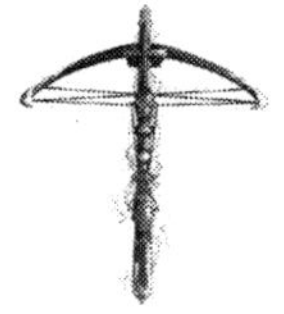

DEFEAT COURSED THROUGH ME FOR A MOMENT, BUT I refused to give up. There had to be another way to keep Rachel safe and not let Silas get what he wanted.

Then, I realized that if Silas didn't have any help, he had nothing. The bastard hadn't once fought against me. In fact, I distinctly remembered him dropping to the floor when Rachel had burst into the room before, throwing blades.

Silas might have looked like he was okay, but I was beginning to think he was worse off than he'd been pretending.

I turned my attention to Caleb, trying to separate my past from the present. The eyes staring back at me were no longer the deep green ones I remembered falling for all those years ago. There wasn't a single part of me that still loved him, but that didn't mean I hadn't kept him in my heart, using him as a shield to keep all others at arm's length.

That time was over. The Caleb I knew was dead. The man I remembered died the moment he became a vampire. Whether that was by choice or force, I'd never know, because I didn't care enough to ask.

Instead, I steeled my resolve and did whatever I needed to do to save Rachel.

"Syn," Caleb warned as he pressed the stake further into Rachel's chest.

"Take it out," I demanded with a snarl and heavy dose of mind control.

He complied too easily, jerking the stake from her chest quickly and taking a chunk of skin from her at the time. I stepped forward cautiously, watching the weapon his trembling hand still held too close to my friend. As I stepped forward, the door to the rooftop slammed open, and I breathed a sigh of relief.

Maciah.

He was there. He would help Rachel while I finished what I'd come here to do.

Rachel used the arrival of our friends as a distraction and rolled out of Caleb's hold. She backed up, seeming to wait for either me to act or the others to appear from around the corner.

As much as I wanted to put eyes on Maciah, I

knew where I was needed most. I knew what I had to do.

I turned away from Caleb and Rachel, giving Silas my full attention for the final time. I charged for him, letting my power build before readying myself to attack.

Except Silas was ready for me. His hand reached out, halting my momentum and lifting me until my feet were off the ground only to slam me down onto my back. My teeth clenched as vibrations from the impact rocked through me, breaking whatever focus I'd been holding on to.

Okay, maybe he wasn't as weak as I'd let myself believe for a minute.

He pulled a dagger from a sheath at his side and stabbed me in the shoulder.

My jaw tensed, holding in a scream as the metal burned like a mother, but I refused to make a noise, giving him the satisfaction of my pain.

Silas grabbed my hair, dragging my body across the rooftop. "You're coming with me."

"Like hell I am," I said, scrambling to release his hold and reach for another weapon.

My nails raked down his forearm, breaking skin and ripping tendons apart. Except, before I could get far enough away from Silas, he reached for me with his other arm and tossed me over his shoulder with the smallest of efforts.

Damn it. He was so much stronger than I'd thought, but that wouldn't deter me. The thought of giving up would never enter my mind.

I still didn't quite understand how the power inside me worked, but I knew it packed a punch as long as I didn't get distracted. I intended to throw as many hits at Silas as I could.

Silas stepped to the edge of the roof, preparing to leap with me in his grasp. I had no idea if he planned to keep hold of me or if he was going to throw me off, but I had no intention of finding out which.

"Put me down," I demanded, pushing power behind my words.

He laughed so hard that the noise reverberated through my chest. "You can't control me."

Rachel had warned me that this ability wouldn't always work on older vampires, but that didn't mean I couldn't continue to try. He couldn't block me forever.

I shoved the power outside of my body, focusing only on Silas, hoping to take away his awareness.

Instead of doing so, he grunted, swayed back and forth, then tilted forward. The edge of the roof was right beneath us, and we were inches from going over.

I knew I wouldn't die from a fall this high up, but I didn't want to find out what kind of injuries I might sustain by doing so, either.

Leaning back, I forced Silas to teeter away from the edge and hit him with another dose of the magic pounding within me, still trying to take over his thoughts.

My hand reached for the stake I thought was still tucked in my back pockets, but there was nothing there. Silas was shaking his head, groans turning into snarls as he fought against the mental hold that I had barely managed to get on him.

There was only one option left. I needed to fight him, just like I would have any other vampire before I was turned.

With a determined mindset, I used my speed and precision to twist myself around from where I was still draped over his shoulder, taking advantage of what little hold I'd been able to get on Silas's mind.

Pushing against his chest, I shoved him back and forced him to crash into an old metal storage container. His eyes blinked rapidly, my power lifting even quicker now that we weren't touching. I wasted no time, knowing there wasn't much left, and leapt from where I stood, closing the distance between us.

As I moved through the air, I caught sight of Caleb and Maciah fighting, Nikki checking on Rachel, and Zeke fighting other vampires at the door. They hadn't been wrong when they said Silas had an endless number of vampires at his disposal. They kept appearing at the most annoying of moments.

I trusted my friends had everything handled and refocused on Silas, but as my arms wrapped around him, he was already trying to twist out from under me.

His hand was reaching for a stake on the ground near us, and I wrapped my fingers around his throat, hoping to tear his head off before he could grasp the wooden weapon.

Silas bucked beneath me, using the support of the metal container behind him to force me backward, but my hold didn't relent. I doubled my efforts, grinning as my nails cut through his skin. But my smirk fell as soon as I realized he'd pushed forward enough to reach the stake.

His arm raised, aimed right for my chest. I dodged left, losing my hold on him and taking a hit to my right hip. I sucked in a sharp intake of air and scowled at Silas.

Gritting my teeth, I channeled my vampire speed and precision before yanking the weapon from my side and, without hesitation, I spun out of the weakened hold he had on me.

As I swung back around, I sent another blast of my power at him, demanding it to stun the vampire. I just need a split second to end this.

Silas hissed at me, blurring forward, but then stumbled as my energy settled over him. His red eyes flashed at me, trying to fight against my will, but his attempts were feeble, and I had no problems taking advantage of that.

Without hesitation, I rammed the stake into Silas's chest, pressing and twisting until I was certain the metal tip had pierced his worthless heart.

His mouth fell slack as I slammed my palm down on the butt of the stake for good measure. His hands pawed at me, but the movements were growing weaker by the second. Silas was going to die, and there wasn't a damn thing he, or anyone else, could do about it. Not any longer.

I stood there, focused and watching until Silas's skin began to fade and shrivel. His eyes paled into white orbs as flakes of skin began cracking until there was nothing left of the terrorizing vampire, leaving a smile on my face.

He might not have haunted my past, but the crazed bloodsucker had hurt people I cared about, killed innocents, and stole lives. There were more than enough reasons for me to hate him and take joy in the pieces of him that floated away in the wind.

As my stake tumbled onto the rooftop and Silas disappeared into ash, a shadow fell over me and a hand reached out. I accepted the offer, turning around to look into the dark eyes of Maciah.

He had a fading pink line across his forehead and rips along the front of his shirt, but there was nothing that I could see I needed to worry about as he pulled me against his chest. “I’ve never been as furious as I was when I couldn’t get to you.”

“You got here exactly when I needed you most,” I murmured, pressing my lips to his chest before pulling back to check on the others.

Rachel stood with a hand held over her chest with Nikki and Zeke on either side of her. There was no Caleb to be seen. They’d killed him, as I suspected they would. I’d thought there would be some sort of grief to feel inside me, but there was nothing other than relief coursing through me.

Rachel nodded at me in understanding. She was the only one who knew that he had been my ex, unless Nikki had also figured it out somehow. I’d tell the others later—more specifically Maciah—but now was not the time.

“Dave,” I said, not forgetting we’d left him in an office, unprotected and dying.

“I sent Eddie to check on him as soon as we cleared the lower levels. I could hear everything happening, but you never responded to my calls through the comms,” Maciah said, lacing his fingers through mine.

“Yeah, mine didn’t survive for very long once Silas announced he knew you were with me,” I said as we moved across the rooftop. I wanted to catch up with the others, but I knew there would be time for that later. Dave needed us more.

Maciah let go of my hand when we reached the door, and I led the way back to the office. The door was open, and I could see Eddie's back with bullet holes scattered over his shirt.

"Jesus," I muttered.

"Silver bullets. That's why it took me so long to get to you," Maciah said.

"How many of ours didn't make it?" I asked when I could still hear the beating of Dave's heart.

Maciah tensed next to me. "Too many."

I nodded in understanding. Even one was more than I would have liked, but I knew going into this fight that keeping everyone alive wouldn't be possible.

Eddie turned back to us. "We need to turn him. He's fading fast."

My head was already shaking before he even finished speaking. "If there's even the slightest chance he'll pull through the human way, we have to allow it."

Eddie grimaced, but I didn't care if this way was harder or more complicated. I knew Dave well enough to know this was not the life he'd want if he had any other choice.

"Let's get him to the car, then," Maciah said, moving in to help Eddie lift Dave.

I backed out of the office, getting out of their way. The pallor of Dave's normally bright complexion was disheartening, but the beat of his heart—no matter how slow it was—gave me enough hope that my bartender would be okay.

Silver ash coated the walls and floors around us as we made our way outside. We'd come with dozens of vampires, but there was only a crowd of eight when we arrived back where we'd parked.

My throat burned with emotions for the vampires I didn't really know. They hadn't died in vain. Silas was dead. Their human lives had been avenged, and I hoped that gave each of them a sense of peace as this life ended.

I moved into the back of the SUV, kneeling on the floorboard and ready to keep Dave stable as they got him inside. Maciah disappeared from my sight as Eddie got into the driver's seat.

I listened for Maciah as he spoke to Zeke. "Have one vehicle follow us and the rest head back to the house. We won't be too far behind you."

Well, maybe Maciah wouldn't be, but I had no intention of leaving Dave alone.

Maciah got into the front seat and reached back to rest his hand on my shoulder. I turned my head to see he had my phone in his hand that I'd left in the cupholder. "Steve left a few messages."

"Thank you." I took it from him and released Dave's limp hand to send Steve a message. The nearest hospital was going to be north of us, so I searched for that first and copied the address into my message, urging Steve to hurry.

TEN MINUTES LATER, WE WERE AT THE EMERGENCY entrance. Two nurses came, but they started backing away as soon as they took in the tattered clothes we were wearing without any injuries besides the ones Dave had.

"You're going to get a gurney and come right back. This man was mugged and badly beaten. He likely has internal bleeding and needs immediate attention. Do you understand me?" I said, blasting them more of my ability than probably necessary considering they were human.

They both nodded and turned, running to get the needed hospital bed.

I gathered Dave into my arms as Maciah appeared next to me, a grimace on his face. "If he isn't going to make it, do you want me to…"

I wished Dave was awake to ask him that question. I didn't feel right choosing for him.

"What about Steve?" Eddie asked as the nurses arrived with the gurney.

I helped slide Dave out of the back seat and he let out a moan. "Hey. It's Amersyn. You're at the hospital. We're getting you help. Just hang in there a little longer," I said, trying to remain as positive as I could be, even though I wasn't sure he could hear me.

As the nurses sped inside with Dave, calling out to the doctors needed, I nodded at Eddie. "Wait out here for Steve. We'll let him decide." Then, I turned to Maciah. "I'm not leaving Dave here alone."

"We'll wait, then." Maciah laid his hand at the base of my spine, guiding me forward.

We followed the nurses, and I averted my gaze from as many of the hospital staff as I could. When we were in the room where the doctor was evaluating Dave, I used more of my mind control, making them stop asking questions and encouraging them to get to work.

"Dave!" Steve's voice screamed from the hallway. I darted out and waved my arm.

Steve was in tears, rushing toward me. His arms enveloped me for several seconds before he looked left and saw Dave. "What did those monsters do to him?" he sobbed.

"I don't know, but we're going to make sure the doctors do whatever they can for Dave," I said softly.

Steve squeezed my hands tightly as the doctors continued to do their thing, talking about emergency surgery and blood transfusions. "I can't lose him, Amersyn."

"Did Dave ever talk about what he'd want if

something happened to him at work?" I asked, trying to lead the conversation without saying too much.

"We wanted forever together, no matter how we had to make that happen. If he needs to become something else to live, then do it." Steve let go of me and went to Dave's side as a nurse began to wheel him out of the room.

I grabbed on to the doctor's arm and pointed at Eddie. "That man isn't to leave this patient. He will be in the operating room no matter what anyone says."

A haze fell over the doctor's blue eyes before he blinked and nodded. "Okay."

I released him, then turned to Eddie. "Don't let him die."

Eddie nodded and quickly followed after them. I did nothing more than watch them disappear around the corner.

Maciah wrapped an arm around my shoulder as we stood in the hallway. "It could be hours before he's out of surgery," he said.

I leaned my head against his arm. "Let's go home." I trusted that Eddie would call when there was something to report. We had vampires to check on at the nest. They'd just lost a lot of members, and I knew Maciah wanted to be there for those left.

A vampire I didn't recognize was waiting for us, parked right behind the SUV we'd arrived in. "I'm going to park this for Eddie to use later. I'll be right back," Maciah said before kissing my head.

"I can take care of that and stay here to wait for Eddie, unless you need me to drive you back to the house?" the vampire said as he came around the front of the other vehicle.

Maciah shook hands with him. "Thank you, Nick. Call me if anything changes."

A weariness settled over me as I glanced back at the hospital, then got into the front seat. We'd killed Silas, but the cost had been high. It was going to be a long recovery for the nest, but I knew there was only one way to heal from the losses.

We had to keep putting one foot in front of the other, doing whatever we could to live for those who no longer did. Just as I'd continued to do for my family, I knew Maciah would do the same for his.

Not tonight, though. Tonight, we'd grieve. And tomorrow, we'd start all over, because our fight wasn't even close to done.

CHAPTER 21

WE GOT BACK TO THE HOUSE THIRTY MINUTES LATER, and Maciah parked in front of the garage. I sat there staring at the metal doors, wondering what the hell we did from there.

The drive back had been quiet. I hadn't known what to say or where to start. I had a lot of questions, but none of them seemed important in the wake of the many losses.

Maciah reached for me. "Tell me what's going on inside that head of yours."

"Too much," I murmured, stroking my thumb over the top of his hand.

He turned in his seat, so he could better face me. "If you're sad about something, you don't have to be afraid to tell me."

My gaze met his in confusion. "Why would I be

afraid to tell you that my heart hurts for all of the vampires this nest lost tonight?"

Maciah looked away from me and out the window. "Because maybe that's not all you're sad about."

Crap. He meant Caleb. I'd known I would tell him at some point, but I didn't think it would be right after the fight.

Maciah had heard Caleb speaking to me. He would have read between the lines on some of the things Caleb said while trying to rile me.

"I wasn't sure if I should kill him. When you hadn't, I didn't know if that meant you might still care about him," Maciah said, voice devoid of emotion.

I reached for his face, turning him toward me. "That vampire was not the man I used to know. I didn't even like who Caleb had become while he was a hunter. I don't know why I hesitated when I could have ended him, but I'm glad you killed him. If there is any sadness I feel for him, it's because of the path he took, not because he still meant something to me."

Maciah leaned his head forward, and I did the same, ignoring the center console digging into my hips. "I'm sorry."

"You have no reason to be sorry, I assure you." There had been a moment when I thought maybe a small, twisted part of me did still care about Caleb, but it wasn't in the way Maciah had assumed. I could see that now, and I hoped Maciah believed my words.

His hands brushed over the two spots where Silas had stabbed me. "Are you sure you're okay?"

My skin was still sensitive and ached if I stretched too far, but there was nothing that could be done for either wound other than wait out the healing process.

"Besides the unexpected appearance of silver bullets, what happened out there?" I asked since Maciah didn't seem eager to go inside. I assumed he thought the expectation would be that as soon as he stepped out of the SUV, he would have to begin the rebuilding process of his nest, but I was certain that there was no one other than him who thought that.

Maciah leaned his head back on the headrest and closed his eyes. "I expected there to be dozens of vampires fighting for Silas, but there were three times as many as we prepared for. Every time we killed one, two more appeared. Honestly, I'm not even sure how we survived. I tore through vampire after vampire trying to get to you. Listening to what was happening up there and knowing you were by yourself, it nearly killed me."

"Your nest needed you more than I did. If you hadn't been there, using your rage, we might have lost all of them," I said softly, hoping to ease at least some of the guilt he was feeling.

"Your power didn't work on him, did it?" Maciah asked, turning his head and opening his eyes once again.

"Yes and no. He was affected, but it was taking more effort from me than it did on any of the others. The mind control played a big factor in me beating the vampires who tried to keep me contained for Silas."

Before he could respond, a humming sounded in my ears. "Do you hear that?"

Maciah nodded, rolling down his window. "It sounds like something is flying overhead."

My stomach churned with nerves, and I reached for the handle. Maybe it was nothing, but I didn't want to assume. Not after the night we'd had. Silas could have had contingencies if he lost.

Maciah followed my movements and I met him at the back of the SUV. My eyes searched the sky, looking for whatever was making the sound.

"There's more than one of whatever is up there," Maciah whispered as we focused.

I pointed. "Is that a drone? Is someone spying on us?"

Maciah picked up a rock from the driveway and threw it at the flying contraption. The motor sputtered and something beeped as the drone fell toward the edge of the property line.

We waited to see where it was going to land, searching for anything else out of the ordinary.

"There's at least a dozen more of them," Maciah sneered.

I listened intently, and the hum of more small motors were headed our way. "Should I get the others?" I asked.

Just as I took a step toward the house, the one that had fallen to the ground let out a siren-like noise and flashed red before exploding in a force so strong we were knocked halfway down the driveway.

"We have to get everyone out," Maciah shouted.

I heard a door open and wanted to call out, but it was too late. The other drones were there, and they were dropping bombs. Lots of them.

I gripped Maciah's arm as we got up from the ground, watching helplessly as the entire mansion was torn apart from the explosions. Screams echoed around us, then quieted as tears fell down my cheeks.

Rachel. Nikki. Zeke. Everyone else.

Not a single one of them exited the burning inferno.

I covered my mouth, trying to stifle the sobs that wanted to escape. Everything inside me burned with fury and sorrow while my eyes moved back and forth across the yard and driveway, waiting for any sign of movement.

Please, someone come out, I silently begged as my legs weakened from the distress of watching everything go up in flames. The black smoke and scent of char was everywhere.

Maciah stayed at my side, his lack of movement crushing my soul even further. If he wasn't trying to save them, then that only meant one thing—even Maciah thought they were all gone.

Minutes of tense, grief-stricken silence passed, but still, no one exited the house. When the structure began to fall in on itself, succumbing to the intense inferno, I held on tightly to Maciah who vibrated beneath my touch, frozen in rage and shock.

Silas had indeed set up a contingency plan, and the price of killing him had just been paid.

Need to know what happens next? Preorder Vampire Vow, the final book in Scorned by Blood, releasing January 2022!

Looking for something to read between now and then? Check out the rest of the Mystics and Mayhem world beginning with the Broken Court series!

STAY IN TOUCH

Find Heather on Facebook:

Reader Group:

Want to talk all things books and get updates before anyone else? Come hang with me in my reader group!

Heather Renee's Book Warriors

Author Page:

Teaser and big updates are also posted here!

Heather Renee Author

Newsletter:

I send this out sporadically. Don't worry. You won't ever be spammed by me and you get a couple goodies when you sign up!

http://smarturl.it/HeatherReneeNL

ALSO BY HEATHER RENEE

Scorned by Blood

A New Adult Vampire series featuring a supernatural hunter and the sexy vampire bound to protect her no matter the cost.

Luna Marked

A complete New Adult wolf shifter series (dual POV) featuring a strong-willed leading lady and a patient, yet fierce alpha male.

Broken Court

A complete New Adult Urban Fantasy series featuring an unconventional and anti-heroine leading lady, a broody love interest, and a fae kingdom with a vile king.

Royal Fae Guardians

A complete Young Adult Urban Fantasy series featuring fae, magic users, a sweet romance, along with snark and humor.

Shadow Veil Academy

A complete Upper Young Adult Urban Fantasy Academy series featuring shifters, elves, witches, and more.

Elite Supernatural Trackers

A complete New Adult Urban Fantasy series featuring witches, demons, a smart-mouthed female lead, alpha males, and a snarky fairy sidekick.

Raven Point Pack Series

A complete Upper Young Adult Paranormal Romance series featuring wolves, witches, vengeance, and fated mates.

Blood of the Sea Series

A complete Young Adult Paranormal Romance series featuring vampires, open seas adventures, and the occasional pirate.

Standalone

Marked Paradox - A complete Young Adult Fantasy fae story about a realm divided and one fae to bring them back together.

ABOUT THE AUTHOR

Heather Renee is a *USA Today* bestselling author who lives in Oregon. She writes urban fantasy and paranormal romance novels with a mixture of adventure, humor, and sass. Her love of reading eventually led to her passion for writing and giving the gift of escapism.

When Heather's not writing, she is spending time with her loving husband and beautiful daughter, going on their own adventures. For more ways to connect with her, visit www.HeatherReneeAuthor.com.

Made in the USA
Middletown, DE
16 December 2023

45782227R00161